# THE QUEEN THE FAE FORGOT

ANALEIGH FORD    EDEN BECK    SABRINA THATCHER

# THE QUEEN THE FAE FORGOT

# CHAPTER ONE

IF THERE WAS EVEN AN OUNCE OF THE GLAMOUR LEFT IN ME—THE one I inherited or otherwise—blood would have been shed in that instant.

I don't know whose blood, as likely my own as any other, but it would have painted the walls of my uncle's study that uniquely crimson color. I would have made for myself a nightmare I'd never be able to forget, if only to make sure that what I stood in the midst of wasn't a dream.

I'd fought too hard, too long, to get here, to my court, my crown, my family—only to feel as if all of that was further out of my reach than ever. It was so close I could literally reach out and touch it, tilt back my head and taste the scent of it on my tongue, but still, now, it only felt so utterly, heart wrenchingly, unreal.

The tips of my blackened fingertips weren't the only thing that turned numb the minute I laid eyes on my sister, Ada. She was transformed, a version of herself I'd never dared to even hope I'd have the chance to lay eyes on. This was not the child I left behind. This was a woman, a creature now at least appearing to be my peer in both body and mind. She'd changed, transformed completely—and still, I'd have known her anywhere.

Any time. Any place. Any form.

Icarus didn't have to tell me who she was for me to know this creature intimately before me ... even if she couldn't say the same.

I hadn't yet had the chance to see how much my own appearance had changed with the lifting of my mother's glamour, but even if I hadn't changed at all, I knew Ada still wouldn't have recognized me. I'd made sure of that when I used my powers for the first time. The powers that would now, if I had any access to them, perhaps tilt the scales of fate in my favor.

For once.

But as usual, try as I might to fight it, I'd once again found myself on the wrong side of fate.

I couldn't tell if the study had fallen into silence, or if I was just unable to hear anything other than the loud beating of my own heart. Behind me, I felt the presence of Shiel, Zev, and Finch, their bodies as rigid as my own felt. Their hands still grazed the metal of the swords strapped to their hips, not because of Ada, however, but because of the presence of the dark fae lord we'd thought broken. Here he stood before me now, however, whole, no sign of the injury that had left him a hollow shell of himself only days before. All of him towered over me, smirking down from barely the distance it would take to reach out and touch him, too.

For a second, the smallest of shivers raced down my spine at the thought. His touch would be all too familiar to me. I had memories of touching Icarus that were far from holy, but the unholiness of my current thoughts had taken a far different turn. My current desire was not to touch Icarus with the blackened, numb tips of my fingers, but rather with the pointed tip of sharpened steel.

I and the fae I'd brought into my court were not the only ones, it seemed—for when the silence was broken by my flaming-haired uncle, Eckhardt, it was with one of his own hands already wrapped, white-knuckled, around the hilt of his sword.

"What kind of farce is this?"

His ire, however, when I turned to look at him, was not fixed on me.

He looked, instead, between the queen and Icarus, his eyes narrowing by the second even as his fingers tightened their grip.

"There's no need for swords, anyone," the queen said, though from the look on her own face as she once more glanced over me, if *she* had one at her side, she'd be reaching for it too. "We're all friends here."

*Friends.*

The very idea was so laughable that if I hadn't been so completely numbed, I would have burst out like the madwoman I was well on my way to becoming.

At least, it seemed, I wasn't the only one.

Eckhardt's lip curled up in disgust as his eyes once more took in the shape of Icarus, standing above us all with the imposing curl of those horns twisting even higher than his already impressive form.

"Forgive me if I'm shaken by the appearance of one changeling in this court today," he half growled, "but has all the rest of this world lost its mind as well? Since when was

3

the dark fae allowed to enter the gates of this city at all, let alone walk as a guest amongst the palace halls?"

Icarus' gaze drifted ever so lazily over towards my uncle, with only a single twitch of the muscle of his jaw to reveal the captain's words had any effect on him.

That single twitch was enough, however.

I heard the slight grate of steel as three sets of hands tightened on their own hilts, too, behind me, the blades itching to be fully freed. I was sure if I looked at them, their knuckles would match those of my uncle, still struggling not to draw his own blade.

Unsurprisingly, the only figure present that actually seemed completely oblivious to the tension coursing beneath the surface of our exchange was Ada. My sister stood looking only slightly bored as the fates of three faerie courts hung in the balance before her—and in extension, all of Luxia.

I myself was torn, pulled in so many directions all at once that I hardly retained the capacity to breathe. I desperately wanted to demand of Icarus what this latest game of his was, how he'd created this golem of my sister—for that was what she had to be—but I found myself unable to ask it in front of her, even as I tried to convince myself that this creature, this version of her, couldn't really be *her*.

Could it?

Though I couldn't bring myself to believe my eyes, I couldn't bring myself not to believe them, either.

Ada might not remember me in any way, in any form, but the last thing I desired was to make her distrust me now that we had the chance to become reacquainted.

If it was her, after all.

It was with the same unspoken question that my mother's

gaze once more flickered in my direction. Her eyes met mine, only for a second, before flitting away almost as if in shame.

Or perhaps not shame, perhaps the same disbelief that kept mine from meeting my sister's.

We were at an impasse, stuck three ways at once. Every hand that had access to a blade already held it. A thousand unsaid words hung between us, distrust and fear thick enough to slice the moment one of those blades was drawn. And drawn they would be, if something didn't change—and fast.

Not for the first time, the only thing standing between a war of the courts was the dark fae lord smirking down at the rest of this as if this was nothing more than another scene played out for his own amusement.

Perhaps blood would be shed, after all.

# CHAPTER TWO

ICARUS, LORD OF THE WILDNESS, HAD US RIGHT WHERE HE
wanted us.

He might not have had control of my powers directly, but
he held more power over me than ever. He'd found the one
thing that actually mattered to me, the one thing I wasn't able
to risk, even as I struggled to believe the creature before me
was the sister I'd been willing to risk all for in the first place.

That wasn't what concerned me the most, however. What
concerned me the most was the way the queen turned to look
at Icarus as she, along with the rest of us, waited for the
words that would either sate or damn us all.

Icarus let out a low chuckle, the sound sending shivers
down my spine. It was obvious he was enjoying this,
savoring the power he held over all of us, this game of his all
too similar to that of a feral cat playing with an already
exhausted mouse. I could feel his gaze on me, and I shuddered involuntarily. I was no match for him, not in my
current state. But I refused to let him see the mix of emotions
that were churning inside me, the fear and dull remnants of

something more like desire that together threatened to over-whelm me at any moment.

Finally, after what felt like an eternity, he spoke. "My dear Captain Eckhardt, though our past ... interactions ... may have led you to feel otherwise ... I assure you that I come in peace. I have no intention of causing harm to you or your court."

My uncle narrowed his eyes, clearly not believing him. Once again, we agreed on more than he knew.

"And what of the other courts? Are they safe from your ... intentions here, with us? Certainly, I don't have to remind you that whatever you do here directly affects them all. What you consider to be kind in your own court cannot be said to be so for ours."

A thought returned to my mind then, a memory of the seven fae swinging above my head the day Icarus discovered one of his court had attempted to kill me when I first arrived. It was an image that should have struck fear into my heart, but instead, the next shudder that wracked me was one of heat.

It was a gift, after all, one that I'd come to appreciate with more time spent amongst these creatures so often bent on making similar attempts on my life.

As if reading my mind, Icarus' smirk only widened. "I'll not deny that I rule over my court differently than the other lords and ladies, but I assure you again ... Captain, Queen ..." For a brief moment, his eyes flickered to me, and not my mother when he spoke of the queen, and once again, my body flooded with heat before he continued. "I am here for reasons outside myself and my own desires. My only concern is with the balance of power in this realm."

This time, it was Shiel who's voice growled out. His lip curled up in disgust as his own accusation rumbled out from the back of his throat.

"You know nothing but your own desires," he snarled. "Any fae who chooses to trust a single word that comes from between those lying lips of yours is a fool."

"What of the Oracle, then?" Icarus asked, without so much as skipping a breath. "Do you trust her word?"

The heat that had bloomed inside me cooled as the rest of the room froze.

I wondered if the others' hearts beat as loud as mine now did. *The Oracle.*

I'd known that Icarus visited her shortly before I did, and that whatever she'd told him had caused her part of the Wildness to disappear in flames—a sacrifice for the dark fae that now stood before us all, eyes lit from the knowledge that only he now held and the rest of us desired.

I knew still, somehow, the words that he would speak next before he spoke them. His eyes met mine, his lips parted, tongue darting out for the briefest moment as if he tasted the heaviness in the air between us. In that look I saw the words before they came, felt the way he relished speaking them, heard the crack they formed, threatening to split the courts that gathered before him. Still, it didn't stop my blood from turning to ice as they washed over us, one by one, even though I'd heard them before.

"*A deal once made is now completed,*
*All the royal thrones unseated.*
*What was stolen soon forgotten,*
*At the very core is rotten.*
*Avarath has turned its eye,*

*Heed the cost or you will die.*
*All us now our own Creators,*
*In this court of thieves and traitors."*

I'd heard those words repeated in my mind, in the hellish landscape created by the tea that had last drawn Icarus to me through the bonds of the magic now fully binding me, too. He'd been a nightmare then, the mere image of his blackened, twisted body as painful as any poison running through my own veins.

The sound of the oracle's words issuing from Icarus' lips felt like a poison of their own, too. They wound around me, seeped inside me, steeped me in their own special venom. They were words had had long since begun to haunt me, even before I knew what they were—and yet, still, I knew not what they meant. Not truly.

Though, from the look that flickered between the dark fae and the others now gathered before me, I almost wondered if that, too, was about to change.

It was Eckhardt who let out a low growl. "A prophecy," he hissed. His eyes flashed an even brighter blue, the deep tone of his voice making the hair at the back of my neck stand up straighter with each rasping word. I didn't understand the anger in his voice, but what I did understand was the fear that shook the next to break the silence.

The queen shrunk back slightly, her own gaze darkening as her eyes glazed over. "Not a new one," she said, her tone softening until it was almost inaudible. Almost.

It wasn't soft enough to keep Icarus from hearing, and certainly not enough to keep him from acting.

"No," he agreed, stepping forward slightly again. "One long forgotten. But not by all ..."

Not for the first time, every eye in the room turned to me. This time, however, the weight of it had shifted.

"Unless my memory fails me, Aurra was the first one here to be reminded of the prophecy," Icarus continued. "Her visit to the Oracle, it seems, served to dredge up old wounds that were too long forgotten."

*The first one?*

Had Icarus been back, then? What price had to be paid the second time?

There was always a price.

My gaze flickered over to Ada—or her imposter—as I remembered my own, a price I was still paying.

Then again, he could be lying. Perhaps I'd told Icarus more than I remembered when I called him to my side in my tea-addled state.

Whatever the truth of it, now was not the time for more lies. Not from me. Not if I wanted answers.

I glanced at Eckhardt before I spoke, checking to be sure that the tip of his blade wouldn't next be pointed towards *me* if I did. I'd heard his warning when he first suspected my power and seen the truth of it in his eyes. He was a fae that knew too closely the glamour I possessed in all its unholy glory.

After a long moment, my uncle nodded, however slowly, his careful gaze never leaving mine.

"Tell us, Aurra," he said, the tone of his voice as dangerous as it was the moment he first threatened my life for the use of my voice. "Or else this insufferable monster will do it for you, but not without weaving into it his own web of lies."

I only allowed my gaze to flicker away from the sword now

pointed at me for a second, and only long enough to wonder if I'd imagined the frustrated look I thought I saw flicker across Icarus' face. It was so brief and so subtle that I couldn't be sure I'd seen it at all, or if I'd simply imagined it—that I had *wanted* to see some sign of it so badly that I'd dreamed it up completely. Maybe, because if he did show some sign that my uncle's accusations had wounded him, then maybe it would make that same monstrous accusation a little less true.

Even if one glance at my sister, at Ada, only confirmed it was. Icarus was a monster. That was not a question.

But I wasn't.

Not yet.

"What Icarus claims, it's true," I said, finally. My voice came out broken when it issued from my lips. Each word made my heart race faster as my hands grew clammy and slick with sweat. I took a deep breath, trying to steady myself as I continued. There was no conscious reason for the nerves that now tangled within me, but tangle they did. "I didn't know it was a prophecy when the Oracle told it to me, but even then … even when we did …"

I glanced towards Shiel, my words failing me as I searched his face for some sort of confirmation that I was doing the right thing. My uncle was right, I knew that I couldn't just let Icarus have his way with this, but I didn't want to reveal something I shouldn't. The words alone, repeated as if from my own nightmares by the dark fae, were enough to elicit a reaction from both my uncle and the queen. They'd heard them before, I was willing to guess.

But what I wasn't so willing to guess was whether or not I should share the rest of what the Oracle told me, not when I saw the slight shake of Shiel's head, so subtle no one else would have noticed it. No one else knew to look for it.

The prophecy, after all, was not the most important information the seer had granted me. Not right now, not standing before the fae that had not only so willingly given me up, but had done it with all the spite she could muster.

I felt my voice trail off, fully ready to leave what little I'd already said as my answer until I saw the way Icarus quickened to add to it, the flash in his eyes telling me I'd set him up for something.

So, instead, I took another risk.

"I had a vision," I said, the words tumbling out of me before I had the chance to consider them. They had their intended effect, the words Icarus himself had planned to speak stopped before they made their own appearance. To keep it that way, I continued on—refusing, at the same time, to look at Shiel in case he was once again shaking his head.

"I had a vision, when we were visitors in the Southern Court."

The glance exchanged between the queen and Eckhardt was nearly enough to make me stop. *Another secret revealed before its time.*

There would be repercussions to sharing that bit of information, I was sure, but for now, at least, it gave me one of my own. For all her vitriol in the moments that we left her court, Lady Phyrra had not betrayed us to her sister. I'd have to tread carefully from here on out to make sure I didn't betray her instead.

"I saw the prophecy unfolding before me," I said, drawing attention back to the words that had poisoned the air around us. "I saw the fae entering this realm, saw their triumph, and I saw their downfall."

I glanced once, this time at Icarus before I continued, chin jutting forward slightly as I forced my voice to steady.

"I saw *our* downfall."

*And at the center of that downfall was me.*

That part, fortunately, I managed to keep to myself. I wondered, however, from the way that Icarus looked at me, if he knew it, too.

I remembered, still, the images that had prompted me to call on the aid of the Lord of the Wildness, how my darkest moment had drawn him to me, drawn my power out from beneath the spell that bound it. That image was seared in the back of my eyelids, that image haunted me every time I closed my eyes, the shapes of the bodies piling ever higher and higher, reaching up so close that soon, I was sure, they would finally eclipse that blood red sun.

"Indeed."

It was the queen who spoke. Her face had gone almost blank, resolve the only thing now visible on her features.

"It's not the first time I've heard this prophecy," she said. "Most fae have, at some point, heard it in the form of the nursery rhyme once written from it."

A small swell of something deceitfully like pride welled deep inside me, if only for a moment. It was that same children's story that had prompted my vision, the remembrance of the Oracle's words that had made me finally share them with Shiel and the others. I'd delved into that library to find some common bond with the fae blood I now knew ran through my veins, and somehow, I had. For once, I felt connected to that blood in a way that warmed me even when circumstances gave it no right to.

The queen's voice rose a bit, as if bolstered by the steady gaze those around her held.

"The prophecy is not the only one of its kind, but it is one often forgotten, often … overlooked … due to its nature."

The last word tangled on her tongue, twisting almost into a snarl before she continued. "That is because this prophecy speaks of a great change, one that most fae are not ready, or are not willing, to face. It's haunted our halls since the moment we arrived on these shores, but as with anything else … with time … the fear those words once held has dwindled. They fell into memory, and then, slowly, that memory fell away, too."

"Until now."

She steeled herself up for a moment. "Our forebears left the faerie realm in shambles, made a deal with the glamour that they did not deserve, knowing that one day we would have to pay the price. I wish I could say that day had not yet come, but …"

Here, it was Eckhardt she looked at first, and then slowly, with all the hatred I'd once expected to find in her, she finally looked at me.

"But I think, at last, it has."

The room once again fell into silence, save for the soft rustle of Icarus' wings. I could feel the tension coiling around us like a snake, though whether it planned to strike, or simply to squeeze the life from us, I didn't know.

Something shifted in that silence, and resolve was the mask that once more fell over the queen's features.

"Nothing good will come of any rash decisions made here

today," she said, suddenly, drawing herself alongside my uncle, whatever look they'd shared once again uniting them as a single force. "For now, you have all given us much to discuss."

A subtle flick of the queen's wrist made her meaning clear. *In private.*

Eckhardt moved without a moment's hesitation, his hand reaching for a pulley on the wall that would call servants—or soldiers and more swords—to our side in an instant.

But while her court was used to obeying her, the fae of others were not.

"No."

It was the first time Shiel had spoken in some time. He'd held his own tongue as long as he could, however, and with it, it seemed he was barely able to keep his simmering temper in check.

I was surprised, slightly, that it wasn't Icarus who interrupted. But then, while he would never accept that sort of dismissal in his own court, he was a fae lord used to being dismissed outside it.

Shiel, however, was not.

"None of us leave here until our business is finished," he demanded. "Or have you forgotten who we are? What we are here for?"

The queen summed him up slightly, if only for a second.

"I've not forgotten anything, Lord Shiel," she said. "Some things do not need to be spoken aloud to be understood … however, for all of us gathered here, why don't you do us the honor of speaking, plainly, what you are here to accomplish?"

"Then, at least," she continued, with a sigh so dismissive

that it made color bloom in Shiel's flesh, still gray from injury, "we can all be sure we're on the same page."

Shiel, to his credit, managed to steel himself up to his full height. If it weren't for the still-gray pallor of his skin, despite the ruddiness that his anger had brought to it, I might not have known how close he truly was to collapse.

His injuries were even more grievous than mine. Mine ran through the emptied channels of my glamour, exhausting me, draining me of power. His ran through his veins, draining him of life.

"It's plain what you plan to do, this guise of yours too transparent," he said, through half-gritted teeth. "But we'll not be swept aside, imprisoned willingly in this palace at your whim. You ask what it is we came here to accomplish? Well, let me answer that *plainly* enough for you."

He stepped forward ever so slightly, tightening that noose of tentative peace until it was tight enough to strangle all present, and then, somehow, drew it even tighter with every word he spoke next.

"We did not come here in peace, we came here to conquer," he snarled. "We came here to claim Aurra's crown."

They were words brash enough to ignite a war, but instead of flying into a well-deserved rage, the queen simply turned to me and nodded, her face completely unphased by Shiel's outrageous demands.

"Then take it," she said, so simply, I didn't understand the meaning of her words at first. "If you are my daughter, then the crown and this kingdom are yours to take. But … if you are my daughter, as you claim to be, then you must prove it to me, use the power that you inherited from your father, the power of Tongues, and take it from me."

Once more, all eyes were on me.

I saw the flicker on Shiel's face, on Zev and Finch's too—concern that they couldn't voice without damning us outright.

I had no power, none left that I could use. I'd used every last drop that flowed within my veins, and then some. Just the thought of trying to reach for those dried rivers beneath my skin made pain prickle at the base of my spine.

But the only thing more unthinkable was *not* reaching, *not* trying.

This was what we came for, after all. My crown.

And I was being given a chance to simply reach out and claim it.

If only it was that simple.

All eyes were on me, but mine were on them, too. Did the queen know that my powers were spent? Could she sense it? Why else would she issue this challenge to begin with? Surely, she wouldn't be asking me to use my powers if she had any faith I actually could.

The oracle had warned me that this woman, this queen of the fae, hated me—that her hatred for me ran deep enough that she was not just *willing* to give me up, but that she had given me up in a way that would cause me the greatest pain. The oracle's warning couldn't be forgotten, refused to be ignored, but there was some small part of me that couldn't help but wonder if that hatred that had once consumed my mother might have dulled with time. Sure, the fae queen standing before me showed no signs of love for me, but she didn't look like she hated me, either. Aside from that brief moment, that moment when she spoke of the war she'd feared I'd brought with me, she was indifferent, or at the very least, played indifference very well.

Where she could afford indifference, however, I could not.

I'd been plucked from my tortured human life into a new life that could hardly be called a fairytale. It wasn't the endless calloused monotony of the life I'd been given up to, but it was tortured in its own way. We'd been chased, hunted, cornered, and accused. We'd faced creatures, fae, and humans each out to destroy us, but from the very beginning, the glimmer that brought me through, that carried me onward, was the promise of something on the other side.

Even before I was sure I was the heir, the long-lost changeling daughter of the fae throne, I at least had the idea to carry me on. Even when I wasn't sure I wanted it, even when now, I wasn't sure still, it was a beacon. It was a future.

It was … destiny.

And now that destiny was here, within my grasp, if I could only reach out with my newly freed magic and take it.

So, despite the pain that blossomed at the very thought, I reached.

That pain scraped through me, dragging like pointed nails rasping through the dry canals of my veins, already stretched and scraped by the magic I'd last used, the magic that had last left Icarus a blackened husk before me. The magic that now left own fingertips smudged with darkness that deepened, taking further root as I tried to draw on the glamour— the one I inherited or otherwise—once again.

I didn't need enough to command an entire fae court, I didn't need enough to even string words together. I only needed one word, one drop of glamour.

But there was not a single drop left. No matter how hard I

reached, no matter how I dug my own talons into those fresh, stinging wounds, nothing came.

Not one word.

My eyes met the queens', and even before speaking, before the words dropped from my shuddering lips, she knew.

"I'm too tired," I rasped, at last. "I have nothing left."

Her eyes searched my face for a moment, reading me with that same unchanging indifference on her own.

"Well then," she said, after a moment, her gaze once more returning to Shiel instead. "Then the validity of your claims still remains to be seen. For *now,* I will retire. You've given us much to think on. And no, Lord Shiel, you're not *prisoners.* You're guests."

Then she looked at Icarus next, and for a moment, that indifference on her face wavered, just a bit, before adding, with an almost inaudible shudder in her own voice, "For now."

There was no point in stopping Eckhardt and the queen as they stepped from the room, their servants and guards slipping in just as quickly to usher the rest of our parties out, too. Somehow, in the shuffle of movement, I was the last to be cleared from the room.

The last besides Icarus, that dark fae Lord of the Wildness.

For a moment, we were left alone in the study, just the two of us.

And a moment was all it took.

# CHAPTER THREE

ICARUS WAS NOT SO MUCH A VISION AS HE WAS A NIGHTMARE.

It was hard to believe that this creature standing before me was the same one that I'd encountered at the edge of the Wildness, let alone the one whose dark wings had enfolded me in the river as he awakened in me a desire I'd tried—and failed—to forget ever since.

His form remained the same, of course. He stood like a sentinel bred for power and precision, the hardened muscles of his lithe body visible beneath the drape of his dark clothes. He was built differently from the muscular fae warriors of the Western Court that had finally led me to the place they'd promised, but there was no doubt he contained the same power. Even without the magic he possessed, the twisted magic of his court paled in comparison to this new—or very *old*—glamour that he commanded with more skill each time we had the misfortune of laying eyes on one another.

For me, it had only been days.

But something told me, from the hungry, distant way his eyes roamed over me, for him it seemed much longer.

I couldn't help but shiver as his eyes finally met my own. Inside his dark gaze, I saw all the hunger and desire that had been simmering beneath the surface between us since our first encounter. It had become, once more—perhaps more than ever—a raging inferno. Despite his treachery, his betrayal, his cruelty, there it was, unmistakable, threatening to consume us both. I could feel his power pulsing through the air, crackling with an intensity that left me breathless.

"Icarus," I managed to say, my voice barely above a whisper. He took a step closer, his eyes never leaving mine, even as I continued. "Icarus, you have no right to be here. What do you think—"

He didn't allow me to finish.

"You have no idea how much I've been waiting for this moment."

His voice was low and dangerous. It plucked at a new kind of danger, pulled the strings of something that sparked a different kind of fire between us.

I swallowed hard, trying to push down the fear that was clawing at my insides. I knew that I was no match for Icarus, even with all my own power intact, I was laid bare before his mastery. If he chose to end me now, there would be nothing I could do to stop it.

But even as the thought crossed my mind, I felt a strange sense of calm wash over me. It was as if a part of me had already accepted what was about to happen … because I knew, deep down, that if Icarus simply wanted to kill me, he already would have.

That meant only one thing.

Icarus needed something from me, still.

"What are you here for, really, Dark Lord?" I asked, using

the twisted title Finch had lent me. "What have you so desperately been waiting for? Surely, you're not here to offer another all-too-altruistic warning of omens and oracles."

Icarus smirked, his eyes glittering with a twisted amusement. "I have my plans, my designs," he said, eyes bearing into mine with enough intensity, it almost felt as if his mere glance was enough to glamour me. "But above all that, I have my *desires.*"

The door behind him, abandoned only for a moment, began to open—only for Icarus to throw back his arm, and with a mighty force, sealed it shut again. From the groan of the wood, it was a small wonder it didn't shatter.

Before I could react, Icarus lunged forward, his hands gripping my waist as he lifted me off the ground. I gasped, my hands instinctively clutching at his shoulders as he pressed me up against the wall. His lips crashed down on mine, rough and demanding, and for a moment I was lost in the sensation. It was a brutal kiss, the kind that promised to leave my lips bruised if it weren't for the sudden way the dark fae stiffened.

It was a moment later, still, when I realized why.

It wasn't until my feet were once again firmly planted on the ground and Icarus had begun taking a step away, that I realized why. His eyes still remained on mine, but with a new kind of frustration in his eyes as I discovered the weight of the blade I held now firmly pressed to the dark fae's stomach.

Icarus' lips pulled back with a snarl. "Once again, Aurra, you surprise me."

I'd surprised myself.

At some point in the shift of footsteps, a blade had been pressed into my hand. I hadn't seen who'd done it—Shiel or

Zev or Finch—but whoever it was, I owed them my gratitude. They had the foresight to protect me even when I didn't know I'd need the ability to protect myself. I'd taken the weapon on instinct, not even registering the shift of weight as it was given to me.

But at least, somehow, the part of me that was still desperate to survive this new cruel, fae world had the presence of mind to wield it.

Without my power, however new they might have been, I felt naked. Stripped. Exposed.

I'd have thought it strange, how quickly I'd come to rely on that dormant strength, if I hadn't felt just that. The strength. One taste of the power I now held at my fingertips, as untrained as I might be, was enough.

Besides, that power had always been inside me, always running beneath the surface, just waiting to be released. So, for the first time in my life, I was truly, fully without it.

Even that, however, couldn't explain the enormity of the dread that consumed me now that I faced the dark fae on my own, truly faced him, for the first time since we'd found ourselves entwined beneath the canopy of his courts' sky. Even with the tip of that blade so advantageously placed, it wasn't enough of an advantage. There was no advantage great enough to fully protect me from the creature at the end of my blade, but still, my grip on the hilt of my sword tightened, my knuckles turning white as I stared down Icarus at its end.

However close I'd been to be being consumed by that undeniable passion between us, there was one thing I couldn't deny. Not for a moment, not even with the way my body reacted still, standing so close to him.

He had once been mine, or close to it.

But now he belonged to another, and not just any other.

The reminder of my sister was what it took for the fire in me to burn hot with hate once more, now, instead of lust.

*Ada.*

"How *dare* you."

The words growled out from between teeth gritted too tight, so tight that my jaw ached as I struggled—and failed—to unclench it.

This fae before me was more than just my sister's betrothed. He was her captor. He was a thief of her childhood, of her innocence, her very being.

He was the one responsible for Ada's transformation, or perhaps worse, the theft of her likeness.

"Release her," I growled again, my voice now the one so low and dangerous. "Undo whatever curse you've placed upon my sister and let her go."

Icarus chuckled, the sound like nails on a chalkboard. "Oh, my dear, you truly have no idea what you're dealing with."

"I know enough to know that you're a monster," I spat back, stiffening my grip on the sword once more. "And I won't let you hurt her any more than you already have."

Icarus took a step forward, his eyes glowing with a sickly green light. "You're in no position to make demands, Little Queen."

*Little Queen.*

The sound of the title, however coolly said, made my skin prickle. I bristled in reaction to the sound of it, as if he'd used a slur.

Of course, he noticed.

His head dipped slightly, though his eyes never left mine.

It was all I could do to keep from letting him completely unnerve me.

"I'm in the only position to make demands," I said.

No sooner had the words slipped from my lips, however, then the room was filled with the grating metallic sound of my sword as it was knocked from my hand to clatter to the ground. Icarus did it so swiftly, so easily, that I hadn't realized he'd done it until once more, there was nothing at all to stop our bodies from pressing together.

But this time, Icarus didn't fill the gap. Only his hand lifted to trace my chin, the tips of his fingers teasing almost up to my bottom lip as he gently lifted my face up to look at him once more.

That bottom lip quivered as I forced my question, the one that had been nagging me from the moment he announced his presence, before it could be drowned out by that once again so treacherous beating of my own heart.

"Is it really her? Tell me, truthfully, Icarus." I asked, swallowing hard. "Is she really Ada, or is it some horrible creature made to look like her?"

"I think you know the answer to that," Icarus said, looking down at me with hooded eyes. "What use would an imposter be here?"

"What is your real purpose here, then? Are you here to usurp me?"

"And what would be the point of that?" Icarus asked in return. He once again closed the gap between us, but not with the passion and heat that had consumed that space before. "It's not your sister that I need, it's you."

It was still too much to wrap my head around.

"But … how?"

The outer corner of Icarus' mouth twitched up as his fingers flexed slightly, as if he'd been waiting far too long to be asked just that. There was an excitement in his voice that he couldn't hide when he spoke, a barely contained pride at his newest handiwork.

"You've not been the only one busy since we last saw each other."

Once again, the image of Icarus when I called to him resurfaced. I'd wondered what kind of magic could do that to a fae. I knew little of the glamour, but still, I doubted even Shiel or the others would understand what Icarus was now claiming.

Before I could ask, Icarus leaned towards me.

"Your sister has not had her time stolen from her," he said. "She's lived a full life, she's wanted for nothing. I thought that would make you happy."

Still, I could do little but shake my head in confusion. "Happy that you've forced her to be here, with you, as your … your …"

"Your sister is here of her own free will, I can assure you that," Icarus said. "I'm a monster, still, that remains true. But some lines even I will not cross. You should remember that, even now, after all the time that's passed between us."

If it weren't for the wall now, once more pressed against my back, I would have stumbled back a step. For a moment, a look flickered across Icarus' face, a look that was deceptively revealing for the dark fae. It was a haunted look, a hollow look.

"All the time …"

That look that clouded Icarus' face darkened. "I didn't

heal from that magic in the span of a few days, Aurra ... though you'd be surprised what magic you can reach for when you truly need it," he said, that dread in his face seeping into the tone of his voice now, too. "But no, in the end, it took far longer than that. So much longer. And I don't mean weeks or months." His eyes bored into mine when our gaze once again met. "And all that time, there was one thought that never left my mind. In all that time, I thought often of those last moments I laid eyes on you, *truly* laid eyes on you. That was what grounded me, even in the longest of my dark hours."

Something about his voice, his face, that look in his eyes ... it burned away the last of the doubt that I'd clung to. I knew he told the truth, or at least, the version of it that was true to him. He could claim all he wanted that my sister was here of her own free will. He could say that whatever strange magic he'd used to grow her into a woman instead of a child had not deprived her of a full life. He could even tell me that I was on his mind this whole time—a time that, from the pain in his eyes, was years in the making.

Claim all he wanted, I couldn't help the deep unease that refused to unseat itself where it had settled within me.

This was, at the end of it all, just a game to him.

Every part of it was just that, a part of a greater scheme.

Still, despite all that, I was unable to keep from falling for the latest of the bait he'd laid.

"What exactly do you dwell on?" I asked. "When you think of the last time we were together?"

His answer was too quick.

"You, naked in my bed."

"I wasn't naked—" I started, too soon.

I was right, of course. I'd played right into his hand.

His head dipped lower, his voice all velvet. "Naked enough, then."

Despite the betraying blush that burned my face, my own tongue at least remained my own.

"I think about how you lied to me," I snapped back, all too quickly. "How you tricked me into submission while you gathered your guard to force me to do your bidding if I refused you. That's what I think about, when I remember."

It was not, however, entirely true ... because the image of Icarus blackened and broken wasn't the only one that came to mind when I thought back on the dark fae.

I'd not often let myself think about the shape of Icarus there before me in the dark, of how he felt beneath my touch, beneath my body. But now, here, before him, despite all the warring, angry thoughts within me, that was the image now that came to mind. That was the feeling that sprung forth in me, the feeling of him and the desire that it dragged back up, unbidden, from some dark, depraved part of me.

Icarus knew this, too, of course.

He took in a deep breath, and despite the fact that we were not within the boundaries of his forest, of the Wildness that had once called so deeply to me, I felt as if he could scent my own truth perfume the air between us.

How could he not, when it was already stretched so thin between my rapid breaths?

A slight, wicked smile teased the corner of Icarus' mouth. His eyes left mine, only to roam the lines of my face as if he was seeing an old friend nearly forgotten, as if he was re-memorizing me.

"I've missed your fire."

This answer, of all he'd said to me, caught me off guard.

I choked on my own response for a second, before finally steeling myself up. "What do you want, a prize for doing an evil thing in the kindest way possible?"

"Yes, perhaps I do."

"Then go fetch your prize. She waits for you just outside that door. If you're telling the truth, and she's come willingly, then that shouldn't be a problem."

For a moment, we stood at a standstill.

The tension between us was palpable again, more tangible than the wall pressed to my back or the ground beneath my feet. It clouded every other thought and feeling until there was nothing at all but me and Icarus, Icarus and me. I'd challenged him, but he'd given no indication whether he was going to take my challenge or throw it back at me. He was unreadable, unpredictable, unescapable—feelings that had grown all too familiar when it came to the dark fae before me.

And still, it came as a surprise when he once more stepped forward and pressed his lips to mine.

It was a kiss both sweet and savage, now, less bruising than the one before—both too brief for me to have a chance to break it, and yet long enough for me to feel the moment I melted into it, into him, before he broke away.

Just as suddenly as it had begun, the kiss ended, and so was the momentary spell that bound Icarus and me together. That brief reprieve from the rest of our world, and all it encompassed, was over before it truly began, and as it returned, so did all the complications woven into it.

"You're right," Icarus said as my eyes opened to meet his again. "Your sister, she's outside ... waiting for me. But you're wrong about one thing. This is not just a game to me. No, it is so much more than that, but you … you will always be a prize. My prize. And despite it all, despite everything, I intend to have you."

With that, his arm flew back and the door unsealed. He was gone before I had the chance to draw in breath, his absence leaving me alone with my own twisted desires.

I'd known I was in too deep from the beginning, but I hadn't realized until that moment that I was already drowning.

# CHAPTER FOUR

THERE WAS LITTLE TIME TO DISCUSS WITH SHIEL, ZEV, AND FINCH what had passed between the dark fae and me in the moments we were alone together.

There was little time to discuss anything.

True to my mother's words, we'd barely all gathered together in the hall, ready to be led away by the queen's waiting guard, before we were, instead, summoned back to her side. This time, however, it was not to some quiet study where we were called. We were brought directly to the throne room.

I'd thought the rest of the castle was impressive, but it was nothing compared to the splendor we found stretching before us. The throne room was immense, large enough to house a crowd that numbered in the hundreds. Windows lined three of the walls, great narrow slits of sparkling glass on either side, leading up to a massive ruby-inlaid spectacle that caught the light of the still-rising run and cast a shattered red and white glow down on the throne before it.

And there, on the throne, sat my mother. The queen's

posture was rigid, one hand outstretched to grasp a glass and ruby scepter. The other clutched the arm of the throne just a little too tight. At her side, my uncle stood, his hair nearly the same color of the rubies set into the intricate glasswork at his back. The two of them wore the same expression of resolve, whatever plan they'd hatched clearly already underway.

I had no idea what to expect.

I only knew that we were not alone with them, not by far.

"A bit much for a friendly chat, isn't it?"

Finch was the one to say it, his eyes darting to the side at the dozen guards marching alongside us—and then up ahead to the other two dozen ready to protect the throne.

Shiel's voice was the next to growl out. "They're certainly making a statement."

The throne room was as long as any of the castle's hallways, the great vaulted ceiling overhead only serving to make the steps of the guard echo with each foot they guided us forward.

It was all I could do to keep the sound of it, and the sight of the two grim, determined faces that awaited us at the end of our current march, from completely unsettling the very last of my nerves.

Despite my attempts to steel myself up, Finch nearly undid all that when I suddenly felt his hand on my waist a second before his hot breath was in my ear.

"So, what did the Dark Lord have to say to you?"

I kept my eyes trained forward and resisted the urge to shrug him off. There was no way I was going to show anything other than the same cool resolve as the two fae before me. Still, that didn't stop memories of Icarus from flashing through my mind, and worse still, blushing heat across my skin in each place where he'd last touched me.

It was wrong on so, so many levels.

He was not only my enemy, but he was now my sister's betrothed. I'd not been the one to initiate that last kiss, but I hadn't stopped him. And I certainly hadn't been able to stop my thoughts from once again wandering to unholy places at the press of his touch.

"Not now, Finch," I hissed back at him, hoping beyond hope that my face didn't blush as red as I felt it burn.

Finch fell back, only for Zev to step up in his place.

"If he threatened you …"

The tone of Zev's voice forced my gaze to the side, where I saw his hand still clutching the hilt of his blade. From the stiff whiteness of his hand, he hadn't let go of the blade since he'd first reached for it.

I shook my head, keeping my focus on the Queen. "He didn't threaten me. Not exactly."

Finch was once again stepping up, now so close that he was nearly tripping over Zev.

"What does that mean?"

"Not now."

This time, it was Shiel who answered for me.

His eyes remained steadily ahead, trained on our most pressing would-be adversaries. "She'll tell us tonight."

His order quieted Zev and Finch, but it finally unsettled me—even where the queen and my uncle's stares had not, even where Finch had been unable to. It made an unbidden anger flare inside me that I'd not felt in a long time, not towards Shiel, anyway.

I knew we were all under stress, that he probably hadn't

meant for his words to come out as the demand I heard. But then again, perhaps he did. Perhaps he'd already forgotten his promises to me, to serve me, to obey *me,* and not the other way around. I didn't like this reminder of the fae who'd first shown up in that town near my home, who'd forced his will upon me without really giving me a choice. Not at first.

Shiel had thrown me off, the careful balance in me tipped towards something more chaotic, and I wasn't able to right it before we came to stop, at last, before the glittering throne.

Even though Icarus and Ada were no longer at our side, their absence was as keenly felt as their presence. At least with the great dark fae towering over us, his shadow could be blamed for the blackness of the tension still stretching between us. Little time had passed since the queen made her first bargain with us, but she carried a new resolve that unsettled me more now that I stood close enough to see how even her eyes didn't waver when she looked at me.

My eyes remained locked on my mothers' as we bowed to her this time, the formality of the throne room bearing me down as if of its own accord. Her gaze was hard, and I knew whatever she was about to say was not the welcome I might have once hoped for.

Before the Oracle told me to expect otherwise.

"Welcome back, Aurra," she said, her voice carrying through the room despite the careful softness with which she spoke. It was clear she didn't wish her words to be heard by any wayward listeners. The guards had been careful to seal the doors when we entered, and even now, two remained outside them to make sure no one interrupted. That too, didn't bode well.

It might not be just to keep anyone from listening to what

my mother said next, but to whatever she *did* next, whatever she might order to be done to us. I felt my own hand tighten on the blade that had been entrusted to me, even though I knew I had neither the skill nor the strength remaining to wield it. If my fate had rested on the fine milling of grain, that would be one thing. But the use of a dagger? A blade? Any weapon at all? I was useless.

I just had to hope that this was not the fate the queen had decided to bestow upon us.

The queen's gaze remained locked with mine.

"I trust your visit with the dark fae was informative."

I could feel the eyes of the other fae upon me as I stepped forward to stand before my mother. I tried to keep my expression neutral, but I knew there was no hiding the tempest of emotions I felt from my face.

I was about as keen to discuss with her what Icarus and I had shared as I was with the others.

"Surely, that's not what you called us here to discuss."

The slightest of smiles tugged at the corner of her mouth, but it wasn't a smile of amusement. It was more like a tic, an expression practiced to hide whatever it was she truly felt, whatever it was that was simmering just beneath that perfect, unchanging surface.

She stood from her throne, the rustle of her gown filling the room as she descended the steps to stand before me. I resisted the urge to step back, to put some distance between us, to hide myself from her scrutiny. But I held my ground, my grip on the dagger tightening. I had to be strong, to show her that I was not the same helpless mortal she had abandoned all those years ago.

"You're correct, my would-be *daughter*," she said, her

voice now as low and dangerous as that of the dark fae that had cornered me not so differently. "We have more pressing matters to discuss."

I felt a shiver run down my spine at the way she emphasized the word "daughter" this time. It was as if she had tasted the sound of the word on her tongue and found it vile, spitting it out as soon as she was able to, and not a moment too soon.

*Would-be daughter.* It was an insult of its own, a declaration of her doubts as much as if she'd come out and called me a liar.

She stopped advancing just before she reached the edge of the dais the thrones were set on, just high enough that even Icarus would have to lift his eyes to meet hers.

"The resemblance between you and my daughter, Fauna, is too uncanny to ignore ... and since my advisors have been unable to detect any illusion on you, even I have to admit that the impossible might be possible." She stopped just for a second, and for that second as she gathered her breath for what she said next, I thought I saw just the slightest shift in her expression. For just a space between breaths, I swore I saw not anger, not resentment, not hate—but regret.

"Changelings are uncommon, but not impossible, either. There is only one way to test your power, to see if you, Aurra, truly are the heir to the throne."

*And my daughter.*

The words were not spoken, but the way hers ended left them hanging in the air between us. I was not the only one who heard her unspoken meaning. Eckhardt shifted where he stood, and even the eyes of some of the guards flickered my way, almost as if they were uncertain, too.

"So, what do you propose?" Shiel asked, at my side.

The Lord, and his Western Court guards, were the only ones among us who seemed completely unshaken.

"By the end of the week, Aurra must demonstrate her ability to perform the royal glamour, to perform *Tongues*. Only then can we know, for certain, that she is the true heir to the throne."

Behind her, I caught sight of Eckhardt pursing his lips. This was clearly not his idea.

"But she already—" Finch started, only to be cut off with a swift jab to the ribs by one of Zev's overly zealous elbows.

"And if she doesn't?" Shiel asked, in his place. His gaze flickered only then, only for a moment, to look at the blackened tips of my fingers.

The queen cocked an eyebrow, a dark look clouding her eyes as she prepared to answer. But before she could, a shuffle broke the silence. Heads of the guards turned first, and then the rest of us followed.

I felt, for a moment, as if time stood still.

I'd yet to have a chance to get a good look at my own changed face, but as I turned, I finally did.

Only it wasn't a mirror I looked into.

From some unguarded entrance, another fae had slipped into the throne room, and there was no mistaking who she was.

I knew in my soul, the moment I laid eyes on the imposter princess, that it was my face she wore. We froze together, both transfixed as we registered each other at the same time. The guards shifted uneasily now, and even Eckhardt and the queen had a hard time not looking between the two of us with a sense of awe.

Shiel, once again, was the only one who remained unshaken. "If Aurra doesn't recover in time to complete the task, what then?"

"If Aurra does not—"

I dared interrupted the queen before I lost the nerve.

"We don't have to worry about that," I said. It was all I could do to force myself to look away from the face that had been stolen from me, along with my powers and my birthright all these years.

But something had welled within me at the sight of her. Something deep and ancient and primal rumbled into veins that had once been so dry that I felt searing pain at their emptiness.

But as Icarus had promised, as he himself and performed the impossible, so now did I. I needed my magic, I truly needed it, and this time when I reached for it, I found it.

I looked back into the turquoise eyes that had been stolen from me, widening now with fear instead of shock, and I felt the command boil its way up the back of my throat. Out of the corner of my eye, I saw the shifting feet turn towards me, saw the stoic faces of Eckhardt and the queen shift, too. Shouts rang out all around me, dulled only by the sound of grating steel.

They'd seen where my attention shifted, but before they could do anything about it, the words poured out of me.

They were wrapped with that strange power, unmistakable now.

"If you are an imposter, then it's time you put yourself out of your misery."

For a moment, nothing happened. Those turquoise eyes bored into mine blinking slowly, bottom lip quivering for a long series of second until, suddenly, she turned and lunged for the tip of Eckhardt's sword, now drawn. She nearly impaled herself on it, too, before he had the sense to draw it back.

When that failed, her eyes grew wide in desperation as she reached for the knife strapped to his side, then, wailing, tried to throw herself from the edge of the throne towards Zev and his sword point, next.

Eckhardt and the other guards had fully caught on to what was happening now, however, and soon more than one pair of hands was holding her in place, simultaneously struggling to keep her from grabbing any of the many weapons attached to their persons while at the same time trying to stop her from throwing herself off of, onto, or bashing herself into anything.

It was the queen's voice that finally rang out above the clatter of armor and muffled grunts that came along with her guard's efforts.

She strode off the dais now, headed straight toward me. I felt Shiel bristle at my side and the other two close in with each step that she took.

"End this, now!"

Her eyes burned into mine, fury painting her face a deep purple. Gone was that perfectly curated, stoic mask.

But she held no power over me, now.

Just as I no longer held my own.

"I'm sorry," I whispered, slumping into Zev's waiting arms. "I've no power left."

Rage, pure and hot, flashed in the queen's eyes, and for a moment I saw her lips part, saw her readied to make the order—but then she saw what I saw. She saw how half the guard had frozen. Their eyes were on me, the look on their faces shifting now, too, as they understood what they'd just witnessed. Slowly, as I looked on, their posture straightened, their feet tilted, and they turned their attention—and the loyalty that commanded—to me.

Whether or not the queen had intended to keep her end of the bargain, there was only one choice for her now.

Her eyes were dead when she once again looked to me, her anger still not fully masked beneath the careful expression now stretching across her face.

It was not she who spoke, however. Her lips were pinched together so tight that I didn't think she had the ability to, that if she did, nothing but vile hate would spew from between them.

So, instead, Eckhardt stepped up. He left the imposter still struggling to follow my order with his men and bowed low when he came to stand before me, too.

"Welcome to the Eastern Court, Your Highness." He stopped for a moment and summed me up, a new look, one I didn't fully understand slowly stretching across his face. "A new era is upon us, it seems, as much as we've tried to avoid it."

# CHAPTER FIVE

I DIDN'T FULLY UNDERSTAND WHAT MY UNCLE MEANT. WHATEVER era he'd referred to, it would have to wait—at least as long as it took me to recover.

Temporary quarters were offered to me and my guests while more suitable ones were prepared, or at least, that's what the boys told me as I collapsed into the first thing that even vaguely resembled a mattress. I was slightly surprised when no doctors came to tend to me, and then even more surprised to learn upon waking that they had—only that they'd not been able to wake me when they tried.

Though, I shouldn't have been surprised.

Not when I learned that it was not the next morning that I'd awoken at all, when they told me this, but nearly a week later.

I'd drained more life from myself than I thought.

Upon first inspection, my body had recovered, the skin of my fingers glowing a tender pale pink. The restored skin stretched all the way up my fingers, well past the blackened tips that I remembered. That last spell, the one that had drawn power from the dredges I'd not thought existed, must have dragged that black color further up my arms. Just looking down at the pink skin served as a reminder of the pain that had wracked through me the last time I'd scraped the wells of my magic, already dry, until I'd found those final remnants that sealed my fate here at the Eastern Court.

At *my* court ... and sealed only for now.

I had no fantasy that whatever lay before me now was going to be easy. I'd seen the look on my mother's face when that stoic mask of hers finally slipped, but more than that, I'd heard the words the Oracle had spoken.

I knew the truth of how I'd come to be exchanged for that imposter princess that wore my face, so try as my mother might to play innocent, this was all a game to her, too. Another game ... this one maybe even more wily than what-ever Icarus played at.

At last, my stirring in the bed drew hurried footsteps to my side.

Three faces peered down at me at once, Shiel, Zev, and Finch—each one trying to hide their worry a little less than the last.

If it were only Shiel that hovered over me, I might not have known he was worried at all. But thanks to Finch, I was suddenly sitting up so quickly that the room spun nearly as fast as my heart now thundered.

"What is it?" I gasped, my voice raspy from disuse. "What's wrong?"

"Nothing ..." Shiel said too quickly, his hand bracing before me, as if to keep me from leaping out of bed—which in all fairness, I was about to do. His face was, as ever, calm and collected—but there was something wrong with his voice that echoed in the all-too agreeing nods of the other two fae at his side.

"You were asleep so long, we were starting to worry," Finch said.

He reached for me too, not to hold me back, but just to let his hands trail along the side of my face. His eyes softened slightly, his hand dropping to trace the line of my collarbone that had appeared as the shift I wore slipped from one shoulder.

Zev's face, meanwhile, had reddened. He grabbed the sleeve and tugged it up—too high, high enough that the sudden movement simultaneously nearly choked me.

"Sorry, sometimes I forget my own strength."

Zev's face was even redder once he, Shiel, and Finch had managed to pull the shift back down into place where it no longer threatened to suffocate me. They somehow did this before my grunted protests could drown the rest of them out.

"The only one who shouldn't be forgetting strength is my mother. She has something coming for—"

My snarl was interrupted as Finch suddenly lunged forward again, one finger pressing to his lips with a hiss. Annoyance flared in me as my aching muscles were startled back into the pile of pillows behind me.

"What is it?" I hissed back. "I was just saying—"

All three fae before me exchanged a glance, but before any of them could speak, Zev shook his head, his own somber face stifling my words this time. I fell into silence as the three of them shifted to the side slightly and he gestured towards the corner of the room.

It took my sleep-weary eyes a second to take in the details of the room around me. It was surprisingly plain, the walls empty save for a couple plain white and crimson tapestries hung on the walls.

That was not what Zev had drawn my eye to, however.

The reason for my sudden silencing was slowly rising to his feet from a chair in the corner.

We were not alone.

A tall, spindly fae stepped forward in silence, each of his steps so quiet it was almost unsettling.

"The queen was kind enough to have a doctor stay with you this whole time," Shiel said through teeth barely able to keep from gritting together.

Finch's eyebrow raised. "Kind?"

Shiel shot him a look and Zev nudged him a little too hard in the shoulder. All three of them stepped to the side again, this time to give the doctor room to loom over me. His face remained pinched and inscrutable as he walked me through his examination, checking my teeth and eyes and the tips of my fingers for signs of the magic that had once gripped me.

He must not have found anything, or perhaps he found exactly what he was looking for. Whichever it was, he didn't say, he just finally straightened up and nodded once before making an awkward announcement that he would be informing the queen that I'd woken.

He left without another word, the rest of us holding our collective breath until we heard his retreating steps echoing down the hallways outside. The other sound that we heard was the clink of armor muffled through the door as whatever guards my mother had placed outside settled back into their places.

Only then did the three fae before me fall into a sort of frenzy.

"We have little time," Shiel hissed, his voice low to keep any words from making it through the door to the guards' ears. "We have to discuss where we stand."

"Where we stand?"

Shiel stopped pacing for just a second to meet my gaze with a steely look of his own.

"Much has happened in the last week, Your Highness."

*Your Highness.*

The title struck me harder than when they called me Princess.

"I'm not—"

"Not officially, no," Zev said.

"But actually, really," Finch said, tilting his head to the side and squinting his eyes. "She's always been the crown princess. Does it really make a difference?"

"For now ..." Shiel cut them off with a glare, "that isn't what matters most. Titles come and go. What matters right now is making sure that Aurra, *our* Aurra, stays alive."

All three of them looked at me with an intense stare, and I supposed I should have felt some sort of pressure at their words, but instead, I just let out a yawn.

The gesture made something almost like anger flicker across Shiel's face. Surprise on Zev's. Amusement on Finch.

"Tell me something new," I said with a tired sigh. "From the moment you showed up, all anyone's been trying to do is kill me."

Or use my power.

Including Shiel.

"We're at a crux now," Shiel said, urgency dripping in every one of his words, though they still barely broke above a whisper. "The queen knows her power is waning. You saw the way the guards reacted when they realized the power you held. It's only a matter of time before the rest of the fae begin to follow suit and follow you, not her—if you were to ever appear to be at odds."

My brow furrowed slightly. "What about loyalty? To the queen?"

Shiel's eyes flashed slightly. "There is no loyalty to anyone in this court except to the one that bears the power you possess. Not really."

He let out a small shiver of a sigh. "Whatever happens, we have to play this next part *very* carefully," Shiel continued. "We can't afford to make a mistake now."

His eyes lifted to Zev and then Finch, where they lingered longer than all the rest.

At first, Finch opened his mouth, prepared to protest being singled out—but whatever he'd been about to say died in the back of his throat. Instead, he sat back slightly and just let out a small, resigned sigh as his shoulders slumped.

"Fair enough," he grumbled.

In whispered voices, Shiel and the others told me what had happened in the days I was unconscious.

The queen had sent doctors to tend to me, their bodies hovering over mine without leaving my side even for a moment. In turn, neither had the three Western Court fae. Not that they could have, if they wanted to.

For fear of news spreading outside of the castle walls, the entire population of the palace had been put into strict lockdown. No fae came or left the castle, and only a select few had even been allowed outside of their rooms—to slow the spread of gossip. The castle's inhabitants were told it was to slow the spread of a mysterious disease carried in by travelers that had forced their way into the city gates.

It was a smart cover, especially when the king was known to the rest of the court to be bedridden with an illness that had left the queen ruling in his stead for months now. Only a select few knew the truth, that the king had long since died and the queen clung to the throne now on nothing more than pretense.

Once news spread of what the travelers *actually* brought with them, the rest of the throne's lies would crumble in an instant, because there was only one way I could possess the power of the king.

"It's a good thing you woke when you did," Finch said, his feet once more taking up their familiar restless shuffle beneath him. "Rumors might spread slower now, between closed doors, but even locking an entire castle in their rooms doesn't stop them entirely."

"Finch isn't the only one who's grown restless," Shiel said. "The queen has to be restless too. She's had too much time to plot and plan in silence. Whatever move she's about to make, rest assured, it will *not* be in your best interest."

I didn't need Shiel to tell me that.

At least, I liked to believe I didn't need Shiel to tell me that.

Very little in my life had actually been done to me in the name of my interests, to say nothing of my *best* interests. I'd been a pawn since birth, a tool used to give others what they desired. Even these fae before me—Shiel, Zev, Finch—who I'd come to view as the closest thing to family that I'd ever had, hadn't acted solely for *me* from the beginning. Even now, sworn to me as they were, I wasn't able to shake the feeling that it wouldn't take much of a shift in this world to make them reconsider.

Shiel was a lord, after all. He could claim all he wanted that he was willing to give up his court, even, but until he was faced with just that, it was only that. A claim. Pretty words meant to satiate me, to get me here, to this place, where I now faced the greatest challenge of my life, yet.

It was a challenge that, according to the hurried glances Shiel kept casting towards the door, I had little time to prepare for.

"The queen won't leave us alone for long. We only have a minute now, so we best make the most of it."

I opened my mouth to respond, only to feel whatever I was about to say die as Shiel bowed his head, for just a second, out of a sort of reverence. All three of them knelt for a second, their hands reaching to touch the hilt of their swords.

"We stand beside you, Princess. Your Highness. Aurra."

All three of them moved slightly towards me as. They rose. Finch was clearly itching to swoop in and leave a kiss on my parted lips, but he—somehow—managed to restrain himself.

Zev, meanwhile, had pressed his hand to his chest, to the place where his tattoo should have already faded, but from the look in his eyes, he still felt the racing of my heart alongside his own.

Shiel's hand reached out to cup my chin, tilting it up slightly so he could once again hold my gaze.

"Everything about our world is likely to come undone in the days to follow. But know this. Whatever that may be, whatever may come, I stand beside you. We stand beside you. I meant the promise I made to you in the Southern Court,

Aurra. My men and I, we make a promise with you again. We will stand beside you to the very end, whatever end that may be."

Surprisingly, I believed it. I believed his promise. I believed him.

I'd once made a promise myself, never to trust a fae.

I was about to break that promise, and more surprising still, I was not afraid.

# CHAPTER SIX

A NEW SILENCE FOLLOWED US ON THE WAY TO THE QUEEN'S chambers.

I was grateful, at first, that we weren't once again led to the echoing cavern of the throne room—right up until we crowded into the far more intimate breakfast salon where I was expected to join her, and somehow found the closeness of our quarters even more intimidating.

The queen's wing was decorated with lavish furnishings, the walls adorned with intricate tapestries that depicted scenes from stories much like the one that had terrified me so much back in the Southern Court. They were as brutal as they were beautiful, contrasting against the bright, crisp white of the palace walls. At least the scattered red of the rubies inlaid into the windows painted the floors and walls with an appropriate scatter of blood-red streaks.

The queen sat at the head of a low table, her posture relaxed in a way that wasn't so disarming as it was unnerving, mostly thanks to her once-again unreadable expression. She was a regal figure, still, with her sharp features and piercing eyes trained on me in that way that seemed to see right through me.

She was a stunning sight, even now, draped in a silk dressing gown adorned with so many jewels that they almost seemed to weigh her down. Her hair was pulled back in an intricate braid, and her lips were painted a deep, blood-red, though the hour was still early. The color had smudged slightly at the corner of her mouth, the red transferred to tips of her fingers, now lowering back down to the rim of a bowl of dark dried fruit.

"Ah, my daughter, welcome," she said, the sound of that so unnerving, too, on her tongue, that it was all I could do to stop the tight tendrils of fear from racing down the full length of my spine. It didn't sound like a term of endearment when she said it. It sounded more like a threat. "So glad to see you're awake. Eckhardt and I had just begun to worry that you might not."

Of course, she sounded anything but *worried* at the idea.

The very sight of me standing before her seemed to disappoint her to her very core, to the place where even the most carefully controlled emotions couldn't stop the smallest of sighs from slipping between her lips as her eyes lifted for a second from mine to the three fae standing at my back.

"And I see you've brought your loyal guard dogs."

I was half surprised Shiel didn't draw his sword at that.

He stood unphased, unmoving, this posture as rigid as a statue completely unaware of the disrespect being hurled his way.

"And I'm surprised you didn't."

The response rolled off my own tongue as I glanced up at

the noticeably vacant space over my mother's own shoulder —the place where my flame-haired uncle usually resided.

When her eyes flickered back to mine, I swore I saw for a moment all that rage and hate that she'd briefly shown me back in the throne room. It swelled up in a single spark, the heat of it burning so bright I thought it was about to burst into flame.

I felt a sudden urge to run, to flee from this place and the weight of her gaze, but I pushed it down. I had come too far to back down now. From the way I felt Zev's hand on my lower back, just for a moment, I knew he felt it too, even if it was just through that bond of ink between us.

His touch calmed me, erasing the momentary panic just as quickly as that spark extinguished in the queen's eyes and was once again replaced by a glare so blank it was almost as uniquely terrifying.

"You should be careful how you speak of what little blood you have left, it's only because of that blood that you stand here, before me, at all."

This time, I did feel the others stiffen.

But before my fae guardians could be forced to defend me, the queen held out her hand and gestured towards the empty seat across from her.

"I didn't call you here to exchange insults, I came here to discuss the way forward. So, please … sit."

When I didn't immediately move, Shiel stepped forward, his hand on my back as he guided me towards the table. I felt a jolt of electricity shoot through me at his touch, and I wondered if he felt it too. It was enough to snap me back to my senses and force me to clear my head as took my seat, however reluctantly, still. My eyes never left the queen. They remained locked on her, looking for any slight shift I could read. I saw nothing, but that didn't stop me from feeling the tension in the air, as thick and suffocating as it had been the day we arrived.

The queen lazed back, her hand reaching for the bowl of dried fruits again as if she only half cared if her fingers found their prize.

She looked over me then in a way I'd never seen before. Her eyes drifted over me, drinking me in slowly, taking me in like a puzzle she didn't know until this very moment that she needed to solve. It was disarming enough to make the hair on the back of my neck stand up. Her hate, her scathing glance, felt more natural than the way she looked at me now.

"My daughter ..." she started again, her voice as slow and syrup-laced as the look that finally rose to look into my face. For a second, the queen's lips parted but her words faltered. When her voice once more croaked from the back of her throat, it was half broken. "All this time, and the girl I raised as my own was not my real daughter."

Her eyelids drooped slightly, the irises darkening as she allowed herself to be lost in thought for a moment. "Forgive me if this isn't the joyous reunion you hoped for. I know I should be grateful for the daughter I've gained, but in reality ... I can't help but feel the pain of the one I've just lost."

That, it seemed, was where Shiel finally lost his own composure. I felt his hands grip the back of the chair behind me so tight the wood started to crack and splinter.

"You really sit here, now, and complain about the loss of a *changeling?*" he asked, anger running so deep in his voice that it came out more like a growl.

"And not just any changeling, but one that you—" Finch's

voice followed, only to be drowned out moments before revealing too much.

"One that you were ready to defend above your own flesh and blood?" Zev finished for him, his own baritone dangerously low—though only we knew that danger was reserved for Finch, and not the queen that lounged before us, still.

"Forgive me again then, for wishing to hold on to the last remaining remnant of my family," the queen spat back. "Or have you not heard yet?"

It took me a second to understand what she meant, and even though I'd known the news she referred to for some time now, for some reason, it hit me differently now. Standing here before the mother who never wanted me and realizing that the father who might have felt differently had only recently passed into oblivion, felt like a loss I'd never known before.

It was different, even, than when I lost Ada—maybe only because in a way, she'd already returned to me. My father, on the other hand, never could.

"The king is dead." My answer was deadpan, emotionless in the sea of emotion that was threatening to drown me, but still it struck the queen as if I'd shouted it at her. Her eyes closed for just a second and she flinched back, and for a second, at least in that we were bonded. "We know."

The queen nodded, unsurprised.

"Few know, but that won't last long. We were waiting to announce it until my daughter—" her voice caught for a second before she composed herself enough to continue again. "Until Fauna manifested the gift. Now, though, it seems we know why it was taking so long."

We sized each other up for a moment, and for that

single, brief moment, I felt a companionship with her—right up until I remembered the one, vital, truth at the core of all this.

*She knew all along.*

This was all lies. All a part of the game.

Remembering that, at least, sobered me.

"So, what now?" I asked, knowing the question was too blunt and not being able to bring myself to truly care.

"Now," Eckhardt's voice echoed out from over our shoulders, causing all heads to turn towards him. "We work together to usher in the next era of this kingdom's rule."

I started slightly at the sound of my uncle's voice, and then again when I saw what he'd brought with him. *Who,* he'd brought.

The changeling princess Fauna half-stumbled, half-dragged her feet behind a pair of unarmed, unarmored guards at either of her shoulders.

Her hands and feet were bound and her mouth gagged—and from the state of her, it was clear why. Scratch marks marred the skin of her arms and face, which, from the bloody remnants of fingernails that even now clawed at the backs of her own hands, had been her own doing. Her eyes rolled wildly in their sockets, the whites turned bloodshot, taking in the room with that same fevered hunger that had overtaken her the moment I made my command.

It was clear she was still on the quest to take her own life, as I'd instructed her to—and without the ability to comply, she'd grown more desperate by the hour.

How long had it been since I issued that command? How long had those hours dragged on with no one to lift it? How long had those marks marred her skin? Fae healed quickly, faster than humans—so did this mean she wasn't fae at all? Or, worse, were those all fresh marks?

Whatever the truth was, there was one thing I knew for certain.

This was my doing.

The sight of the changeling princess brought a new layer of tension to the already heavy air. I could feel the anger and fear radiating from her, even through the gag. Her rage seeped through her very being, radiated through the rattle of her bones. My heart ached for her, guilt washing through me in a nauseating rush. But I couldn't let my sympathy cloud my judgement.

Not when she was still the imposter, still the creature that had stolen so much of my life from me. I didn't know her part in it, if it was merely as another puppet, or if she knew what she'd been doing.

The queen visibly shrank back at the sight of her, despite her best efforts to hide it.

"Surely, Eckhardt …" she gasped, taking in the tightly wound gag digging into the sides of her once-daughters' face, "that's a bit much."

Eckhardt's head cocked to the side slightly and a muscle worked at the outer corner of his jaw, perhaps in annoyance as if her words grated at him, but he did nothing to defy her. He simply made a small gesture with his hands and the guards reached to unbind Fauna's tongue.

The moment the gag was released, however, a string of curses streamed from the changeling's mouth until even the guard's hand that still held the strip of fabric twitched, as if he was considering returning it to its former place.

The curses soon jumbled into meaningless screams as she

began to attempt to bite her own tongue off—and the gag was replaced without the need for a second command.

The queen had straightened in her seat, her face paling as she tried to keep from flinching back a second time.

It didn't matter that she knew this was a changeling, I realized.

*She still loved her as a daughter.*

Bitterness rose up in me as I saw the look that was rightfully mine, the sympathy and pain that the queen should have been feeling for me.

It was an ugly feeling, but at least it numbed some of my guilt.

My uncle, meanwhile, just let out a sigh as he came to stand beside the queen. Her loyal shadow.

"I'd always assumed Princess Fauna had inherited her mother's temperament," he said, shaking his head, "but it seems she picked that up along the way."

It took me a moment to understand what he meant, and then a moment longer to believe my own ears. It wasn't until I saw the look the queen was unable to keep from shooting his way, followed by the stifled guffaw from one of the guards at the door behind me, before I could.

I looked over my flaming-haired uncle with new eyes, if only for a moment.

*Perhaps not so loyal after all.*

It was just a comment, a jest, really, but even more important than the look he shot at the imposter who had taken my place, was the one he aimed next at me.

"We've had much time to think, Princess. Your arrival here has disrupted months of careful planning, months of work put into maintaining peace within a kingdom without its king."

"If you're expecting me to apologize—"

"No." The queen's response was curt and unexpected. "No, Aurra," she said. "But we do expect you to comply."

*Comply.*

I didn't like the sound of that word, and neither—from the shift of feet behind me—did the fae of the Western Court.

"We should have known that there was something amiss. Usually, the power of the Tongues begins to transfer *before* the old ruler dies. When Fauna did not inherit it, we began to make preparations just in case she never did. The power of the Eastern Court would not hold without that glamour. It seems, however, that we were misguided," the queen said, sharing a look with Eckhardt for a moment before she continued. "So now, we've made a new plan."

She leaned forward toward me, hands splayed out on the table.

"Soon you will have a whole kingdom to attend to ... one that needs your power now more than ever. But ..."

I knew what was coming before she said it. The queen's voice was steely and determined, her gaze cold and unyielding as she looked at me—into me—her words practiced and careful. It was a look I had seen many times before, but never like this. This time, there was no room for negotiation, no room for compromise.

What she was about to say had already been long decided, pre-meditated and planned in the hours and days I spent unable to do the same.

"These are troubled times in the kingdom of Luxia," she said, her tone so measured it was almost as if she was reading off a script. "We must proceed with caution. Most rulers have a lifetime to prepare, to learn their role, their duties, their expectations as head of these faerie courts. Ruling a land like Luxia is not a simple task."

"I never imagined it would be," I said. I didn't add that I'd barely imagined it at all. I was so focused on getting here, that I hadn't had much thought for what it would actually be like when I got here. I'd been determined not to be shaken, but as the queen continued, I felt the weight that had first settled onto me when I got here grow heavier.

"The other courts have long coveted the seat of power the Eastern Court holds over them," the queen said, her eyes leaving mine just long enough to catch the gaze of Shiel over my shoulder. "If word of our weakness spreads before you're prepared to handle it, then bloodshed will be sure to follow."

I'd expected the queen to put up a fight, to deny me my crown—but here she was, doing the exact opposite. Though she offered me warning, he warnings seemed fair enough.

It was almost too fair. Too easy.

I was wrong, what she offered next was not what I expected at all. It disarmed me, and though I knew it was dangerous to allow it, I couldn't help it.

"You will be crowned soon, Aurra, mark my words," the queen said, head bowing slightly as her gaze intensified. "But If we can buy some time before then, push off the inevitable shock that will follow news of the king's death, then we might at least be able to stem the flow of that blood, if not stop it entirely."

My eyes narrowed for a second as I took in what they said.

"Buy some time?" I asked. "What do you mean by that?"

She took a short breath. "This is what I propose ... but first ... if you wouldn't mind, my *daughter* ... lift this curse you've placed on your twin. I know you wish her gone, but the crown isn't finished with Princess Fauna yet. She still has a part to play for some weeks yet."

# CHAPTER SEVEN

THE QUEEN AND ECKHARDT AND BEEN BUSY.

They said nothing at all that day in the salon, and at the same time, all too much.

Their words were the flowery words of the fae, practiced word-weaving meant to lead me astray, the proposal they made so simple and straightforward that it surely it couldn't be either.

But it also made sense, and that was why I had no choice but to accept it.

The queen's proposal had been this:

Life in the castle would appear to go on as normal.

For two weeks, I would study night and day beneath a tutor to learn my place in this court, while she and Eckhardt prepared the guard for whatever may come once the announcement of the king's death—and my ascension —broke.

In the meantime, I would place a glamour over the castle to protect us.

It sounded simple enough, straightforward enough, but it very soon became apparent why it was not at all.

First of all, the glamour I was carefully instructed to place, drained every ounce of magic in me once again. It was no small feat the queen asked me to perform, one that left me so lethargic in the wake of its casting, that I had no energy left to argue the particulars of the rest of my bargain.

I didn't fall into a useless slumber as I had before, but it was all I could do to begin the studies I'd promised to dedicate myself to.

They began at once.

However, as the days progressed, it was not the curse I was instructed to lift over Fauna that came to bother me in the coming days. It was the one I was commanded to place, instead.

With the king dead, the only true instruction I could expect in using my gift, the Tongues, could come from those who had most often seen him use it. And unfortunately it seemed there were not many.

The king had been private in his use of the power, and I understood why. I'd experienced firsthand its power, that it didn't need the fae it was aimed to affect to be in my presence. So, why then, would the king risk exposing himself by using it in front of his subjects except when he had to?

The queen was the only fae who'd seem him use it more than a handful of times over the years he'd reigned—a useful detail that she was keen to remind me of as she carefully laid out the exact words I should use to bind the court. More than that, she instructed me how to layer multiple commands so that they fell over the inhabitants of the castle at once, and so that—if the time came that we needed it—we could lift part of the spell I'd cast instead of all of it.

This was part of her strategy too, I knew. It gave her life value to me, well beyond my ascension to the throne.

She made sure, as I cast the glamour as instructed, that I knew I needed her.

By having me bind my court with a powerful glamour, she'd ensured her own power over me, protected her place at my side. At the very least, she'd made sure that I wouldn't thoughtlessly dispose of her. Not when I knew, from the careful way she instructed me, there was far more she held back about my glamour then she actually chose to share.

I didn't mind. I had my own secrets, too.

I knew that I'd learn my powers faster with her help, but I also knew the glamour had a way of revealing itself to me without the need for instruction. I already knew far more about my gift then she could possibly guess.

The queen's plan made sense, but that didn't stop Shiel's warnings from ringing in my ears. My mother was sure to have a plan, and this was just the beginning. This would give the queen and Eckhardt time to try and find a way to push me out, I knew, but what was my alternative? To take the throne and my crown by force with my glamour instead?

I had no desire for bloodshed. I already worried enough about the prophecy that had been not only spoken over me, but given to Icarus to remind me of, too. I was buying the queen time, sure, but I was buying myself time, too.

And two weeks, what was two weeks in the grand scheme of things?

This time, the net I was instructed to cast didn't need to

fall over the entire court—just those residing in the castle. Just those that might have seen, or even heard, of the appearance of Princess Fauna's double.

By the time the courtiers were spilling from their rooms, the quarantine lifted, there was no memory of the strange girl wearing the princess' face that had ridden into the castle gates at dawn. No one would notice now that two of us roamed the halls, even though we still shared the same face. Even if we stood beside one another, I'd commanded the court not to be bothered, and what I commanded, they obeyed without question.

Just as my mother, the queen, taught me as my first lesson.

More than all that, more than protecting me, however, there were no more whispers of the king's death.

Quite the opposite.

My mother and I had made sure of that, next.

By the time the next week had passed, all rumors of the king's health had been dispelled. His health had improved and soon was expected to once again hold court.

It wouldn't last forever, this glamour I'd cast with words that drained me once again … but it didn't have to. It just had to last one more week.

If the queen kept that end of the bargain, of course.

I had no doubt this plan was a guise of some kind, but I had no choice but to accept.

And in my heart, deep down, I wanted to.

I'd already fought so hard to get here, to just *be* here, I didn't want to fight anymore. Not yet, not at least until I'd gained the knowledge I was promised. Knowledge was power, and with the king dead, the queen was one of the only fae I could trust to teach me about the power I possessed.

Not that I could trust her at all.

Not that I could really trust any of the fae I now found myself facing day by day.

Only the queen, Eckhardt, and the fae that had traveled with me were supposed to be spared the veil of the glamour. But there were two others I spared, two others I dared not enchant. My sister, because I'd already caused her to forget me once.

And Icarus ... because something inside me couldn't bear the thought of him forgetting me, too.

If I'd known what was in store for me, however, I might have turned down the queen's proposal in favor of bloodshed after all.

A voice that had become as familiar as the sound of my own breath—though a thousand times as grating—echoed through the room, too loud to be ignored. I wasn't paying close enough attention to hear her exact words, but I knew it had something to do with the Eastern Court's established right to rule. I knew that, at least, when the silence fell and the only sound that fell in its place was that of Phina, my tutor, as she cleared her throat. She stared me down as she waited for some kind of response.

Unfortunately, the only thing the practiced propaganda did for me was cause the palms of my hands to itch for a blade—this time to end myself, if only to end this misery, too.

At my ankles, one of the castle cats let out a mew as it wound around my legs. It was the only company I'd had in days aside from those of my tutor—whenever one of them managed to slip inside during the brief moments the doors were opened for more lessons or meals.

Most of my lessons were like this, so dry and scripted, it

sounded like it came straight from the queen herself, some strange attempt to either bore me to death or make sure that by the time I ascended the throne I'd gone through such heavy indoctrination that I was prepared to be her next puppet.

The queen might have been subtle, but the fae—with their thoughts already clouded by the glamour I'm put over them —were not. I caught glimpses of them struggling against it sometimes, flickers of their faces as they found themselves not able to reach for the truth of something they felt dancing just outside their grasp. It was worst for the tutor, Phina. The glamour I'd cast over the fae here was supposed to make them ignore the fact that I looked like the princess they'd come to know their whole lives, but occasionally, I saw the flicker of confusion as their brains tried to recognize me.

If it weren't for the queen's promise—and my own crip-pling exhaustion after casting my last glamour—I would have given up halfway through my first lesson, citing cruel and unusual punishment. But however hollow that promise now rang in my ears some days after it had been made, I still got up each morning with the rising of the sun and studied well past its setting.

In fact, I'd done nothing but study for seven days now.

I'd not left my rooms once, not received one visitor, not been called back to the queen's side. I'd only just recovered enough for that to bother me, however—a fact I was quickly starting to realize was probably just another part of my moth-er's plan.

Phina coughed sharply again, jolting me from my contem-plation. It sounded almost as if she was fighting an illness, or even perhaps that her own lessons were boring her body to death.

From the slow, methodical way she shuffled through the next couple pages of the book in her hands, I decided it was the latter.

I leaned back in my chair and stared up at the ceiling, wishing that I could be anywhere else but this room.

They were rooms fit for a princess, sure, not the near-sterile ones I'd slept in my first week—but despite their splendor and comforts, it was practically a prison. I'd only been conscious in my old rooms for a few minutes, but at least, in those minutes, I hadn't been alone.

Now, here, in all its beauty, the only company I kept was that of Phina making her own slow suffocating attempt on my life. The queen hadn't dared lock me up like a prisoner in the traditional sense, but she might as well have.

Phina cleared her throat a second time, so as much as I wanted nothing more than to bash my head into the nearest sharp object, I just let out an audible groan and forced myself to tune back into Phina's monotonous lecture on the power of the East's rule. Surely, there had to be *something* she could teach me today that would be actually helpful as a future ruler if I really listened.

But no—this was merely a repetition of the previous five sessions' material.

There was no denying the place my court held in Luxia, but I'd never questioned that. I'd only used my powers a few times now, but that was enough to understand the respect—and fear—it possessed. There was enough power in my glamour that my court could rule over all others despite the fact that only one of the fae that resided within these walls had any glamour at all.

As I often did, when my lessons grew dull enough to rot my brain, I reached deep for the wells of my glamour, to feel how deep it now ran. My recovery had been slow, the glamour required to place the entire castle under a complex enchantment almost enough to blacken the tips of my fingers again, but I'd finally begun to feel an inkling of it return the last few days. I had to reach deep, ignore the prickle of pain to dredge up the sparkle of that magic river, but it was there. And it was growing.

I was momentarily reminded of another pain, and suddenly, a realization hit me that was so heavy, it felt as if the weight of it was suddenly pressing down on me so heavily from above that it might suffocate me before Phina's lecture had the chance.

*No one in my court has magic except for me.*

That wasn't strictly true.

Not anymore.

This time, when I reached for the glamour, I felt for the one that felt like trying to mix oil with water. I reached for the one that stung like salt on an open wound when I took hold it.

*The old glamour is back.*

What had Icarus told me about this glamour? Something about how the magic of the courts had forged deep pathways in the fae, that it made it impossible to harness the full power of the old glamour without threatening to destroy them in the process?

But what about fae that had never practiced the glamour? What about fae that had no pathways ... fae like me?

My attention snapped back down to Phina, my posture straightening as I looked at her more carefully.

Did that mean Phina had access to this new glamour now? Could she harness it, too? Did she even know?

And more importantly … did the queen know?

If she did, that was about to change everything.

I was dragged back to reality a moment later when, as if on cue, a sudden knock on the door instantly silenced even Phina. She glanced towards the door, but said nothing, as if she hoped whoever was interrupting us would simply leave.

But after a pause, the pounding of fists resumed. This time they were much more insistent. Phina released an exasperated sigh and gave the knocker permission to enter.

It was a sign of just how deprived of excitement I'd already become that just the sight of a strange male fae peeking into the crack between the door and the frame was enough to set my heart racing. His eyes glanced towards me for a brief moment before shifting away and focusing back on Phina. I felt my arms tense in response to the momentary flicker of confusion that flirted with his features so briefly any other fae might not notice it, if they didn't know to look for it. I did, of course, because it was the same look I got from every fae who looked at me a little too close.

"I apologize for disturbing you, but there seems to be an issue …" He trailed off, his vision flitting nervously between both of us. "With some of the queen's scrolls …"

Phina remained quiet, her silence enough to set him even further on edge.

He swallowed hard, his brow furrowing as he glanced between us and seemed to be struggling to form the connection hiding just behind that wall of glamour I'd placed. Phina waited a moment longer, but when it became obvious that her silence wasn't enough to drive him away, she let out another, even more exasperated sigh.

"What sort of problem?"

The male fae hesitated before continuing, "Some sets seem to be … missing."

She repeated him slowly, as if unable to comprehend what he meant.

"Missing?"

A chill entered her voice as she looked upon her assistant with disappointment and—unless I was mistaken—suspicion.

"Which scrolls exactly, are you talking about?"

I was probably mistaken, more than likely mistaken, driven so close to near madness by boredom that I was looking for anything that might cure it. But still, try as I might to convince myself otherwise, I couldn't deny the way he shifted uncomfortably beneath Phina's dark gaze, as if he was hiding something.

The longer she waited in silence, the more the male's face paled. He glanced at me again, and again, it almost seemed as if he was trying to say something, but it kept slipping away from him before he was even able to fully form the thought. Our gazes met briefly, and then he hurriedly diverted his attention to the floor.

Phina, at last, decided to put him out of his misery, but only because she seemed to be struggling with the same thing as him. Her eyes trained on him for just a second before settling back on me.

"That's three that have disappeared over the course of this week …" I heard it in her voice, too strained, when she spoke. She stopped halfway through her thought, her brown furrowing now, too as her voice returned louder this time. "That's three ... *three* ... just this week, just since ..."

Once again, her voice caught. She glanced first at me, then at the male now standing more concerned than ever in the door.

She looked away quickly then, uncertain who she was addressing with her anger—or even, it seemed, *why* she was angry to begin with. She stood up abruptly and moved to gather her things.

"I'll leave you for now," she said tersely, refusing to look at me now. "I should take care of this."

It was all I could do to hide the excitement from my voice as I stood and bowed.

"Of course."

She looked more confused than ever as she stopped in the door. She opened her mouth as if she was going to say something more, but again, she just shook her head and left.

The moment the door clicked shut, I sprang into action behind her.

The guards were unprepared for the command that spilled out of me on the way out the door.

"Stay, don't move."

The sting of the command, however simple, lingered long after I'd fled the hallway leading from my rooms, but it did nothing to stop a relieved smile from spreading across my face. Even the cat was left surprised, mewing in alarm as it was trapped behind the door as it swung shut behind me. Any genuine interested I'd had in Phina's missing scrolls was replaced by a far more pressing problem.

This new glamour.

It was a rare moment that I had to myself, and I knew exactly how I intended to spend it.

I hadn't seen Shiel, Zev, or even Finch—him, most surprisingly of all—in days. They were the only few I knew well enough to trust, and so naturally, we'd been separated from one another.

But they were not the fae I sought out.

# CHAPTER EIGHT

I REMEMBERED ALL TOO WELL THE LAST TIME I LAID EYES ON
Icarus.

His rooms were somehow fitted exactly to his taste, a
mirror of the innermost nature of the fae standing before me,
frozen, half turned from the table where he'd been working
on whatever wicked thing he plotted next. It was the only
place in the castle that was not all white limestone and
crimson scattered light. Perhaps it was beneath it all, beneath
the velvet drapes that blanketed the walls and pooled on the
patchwork of dark rugs like shadows reaching out from the
corners of the room. The work of some illusion magic had to
have been used to turn the furniture into dark wood and
shiny black obsidian. Even the fireplace had been overlaid
with stones so dark that they seemed to suck some of the light
out of the fire crackling within.

The Lord of the Wildness had brought some of it with
him, that earthy, musty smell of his court wafting out to
envelop me the moment I threw the door open. It mixed with
the scent of my bathwater, with dried rose petals and that

smoky aroma of the fire to create a near mesmerizing combination.

But now was not the time to be mesmerized. Now was the time to keep my head clear.

Or, at least, as clear as it ever was in the presence of the dark fae.

Icarus turned his head slightly, his black hair falling over his shoulder in a silky curtain. His eyes were as dark as the obsidian furniture, and they glinted with amusement as he surveyed me from head to toe. I straightened my spine, refusing to let him intimidate me.

I cleared my throat, trying to sound as confident as possible.

"Icarus." That single word came out muffled amongst the drapes and dark tapestries that lined the walls. That was not, however, where my mind dwelt.

I couldn't help but feel a shiver run down my spine at the intensity of his gaze as it lingered on mine. He was beautiful, there was no denying that, with his locks of dark hair and sharp features. But he was also dangerous, and there was no denying that, either.

"What brings you to my chambers, Princess?" he asked, his voice smooth as silk.

I resisted the urge to flinch at the sound of my still-yet-unofficial title on his lips. It wasn't the first time I'd heard it, but from him it sounded too strange. When Zev and Finch said it, it was one thing … but for Icarus, it was something else entirely. When the Lord of the Wildness said it, it was anything but endearing. It was just another way for him to exert his dominance over me.

Again.

He knew I'd not yet been given that title. He knew it still remained outside my grasp.

I shook a strange feeling from my shoulders as I stepped inside.

It hadn't been hard to find Icarus. I was almost ashamed to admit that I hadn't needed to ask for directions. I didn't want to alert the guards to my presence, since it was better if no one knew I was out wandering the castle on my own. If word got back to my mother, the queen, or Eckhardt—who was always lurking if not by her side, then somewhere close by mine—then she'd be sure to know what I was up to. I'd promised to keep to my studies, but that was just what they wanted.

And now that I'd started to come back to my senses, it was time for me to figure out what they were really up to. I hoped Icarus might know, at least something.

If he was willing enough to share with me.

If he wasn't willing, then … well … I might make him.

I felt no pride at the thought of using my powers. I had no desire to overpower the will of others, even Icarus. If I could have asked for another power, another way to protect myself, then I'd have taken it in a heartbeat. But for better or worse, it was what I had, and even if it made waves of guilt wrack through me each time I had to use it, I would use it. I was the only advantage I had.

When I had it.

This time, when I stood before Icarus, my veins no longer ran dry. I felt that spark of magic, however small it still was, and felt keenly how different it was stand before the dark fae of the wildness with it in my grasp again.

I felt something else, too, the same thing that had drawn

me to him, led me to his door through winding corridors and twisting stairs. That bond between us remained, stretched thin but somehow stronger than ever.

He'd told me of that bond the first day that we met, a bond of fate he'd called it, and here it was, once again pulling me towards the one creature in this world most dangerous for me.

He was the spider, and I was the fly.

I would remember that this time. Should remember that this time.

But still, somehow, the moment I opened my mouth, I forgot what I came here for.

"I know why you're here," I said, instead.

Icarus smiled, but it was a cold smile that didn't reach his eyes. "You already know why I'm here," he said softly. His smile widened as he stepped closer to me and his voice softened further.

Instead of backing down like every instinct begged me to, I stepped forward and looked him straight in the eye, determined that he understand how serious I was, that he might be playing a game, but I was not.

"No," I said. "Why you're *really* here."

As if to punctuate that, to make him see just how unafraid of him I was, I nudged the door shut behind me, waiting to hear it click before I took one more step towards him. The anger that had been simmering in my veins since the moment I'd entered the room suddenly surged within me.

I thought I came here for answers, but I came, instead, to make an accusation. It was not just the queen I needed to worry about, the queen who would use this new power against me in my own court, with my own fae.

Because Icarus had done it once already.

"You realized I won't let you use my powers, that I've already chosen the glamour I inherited instead of this new one you're so obsessed with," I said, "so you've come to the one place in Luxia that you might find another fae willing—or even *able*—to do your bidding."

I felt my lips curl up as I took him in again, the shadows around him drawing ever tighter, the hollows of his cheeks growing more pronounced as even the circles under his eyes seemed to darken.

"You came here looking for another innocent fae to use, a fae to corrupt in your never-ending quest for power."

That smile of his warmed, and somehow that was more terrifying than the cold.

My stomach churned at the thought. He'd nearly corrupted me, nearly convinced me to give up the greatest power of all, one that only I could possess.

That was what he did. Icarus had been doing this for centuries, longer than any other fae was able to even live, all the while taking advantage of unsuspecting fae who had no way to protect themselves from him. He was a master manipulator and a powerful foe, not someone anyone wanted to cross paths with—least of all me.

But now that I knew what he was up to, I couldn't just stand by and do nothing. My mind hummed and my heartbeat drummed as I looked into those dark eyes of his and felt the weight of his gaze on me like a physical force. Whatever happened next, whatever I expected him to say to my accusations, it wasn't what dropped from his still-curled lips.

"You're absolutely right. Well done, Little Queen."

*Little Queen.* There it was again, even more mocking this time.

"Stop that," I snarled, teeth baring.

It was exactly the response Icarus was hoping for.

"Oh, I'm sorry, do you prefer *My Storm?*"

The sound of the familiar term, the name he gave me in a moment shared beneath the trees, back before my life was marred by prophesies and pretense, had an effect on me it had no right to. Just like that, I was nearly undone. A weaker, more naïve version of me would have been. She almost was, once.

Even now, even after everything, it was all I could do to ignore the way the sound of the name he gave me melted that icy cage I'd placed around the part of my heart that tried to beat too fast in the dark fae's presence.

"So ... you admit it?"

It was impossible to keep the surprise from my voice this time. "You admit you're here to find someone whose powers are untrained and vulnerable enough for you to be able to control them."

He didn't answer me directly, but the wicked gleam in his eye said more than enough.

"That's the aim of all rulers ruthless enough to realize it's the only way to get done what needs to," he said, slowly, purposefully. "But fear not, I'm not on the hunt. Not yet. Somehow you've managed to thwart me without even realizing it, I think."

Once again, I was caught off guard, until I realized the obvious.

I narrowed my eyes. "You're lying."

It was almost relieving to realize it until once again he battled off any sense of familiarity with a helpless shrug.

"I wish I was," he said. "But that spell you placed, for I assume it's your glamour that has this entire court spell-bound, it seems to have stopped any of the fae here from exploring their new ... natures."

*This entire court.*

That wasn't entirely true. It was just the castle—but I wasn't about to tell him that, not when, for once, I seemed to have the smallest advantage over him.

I shouldn't tell him that, anyway. Despite that bond between us that urged me to be his confidant, I was not. I couldn't be. I wouldn't be. Not so long as I could help it.

"How could the glamour I cast do *that*?" I asked, knowing there was, at least, no point in denying the existence of my spell.

"Unless you tell me the exact words you were instructed to use, then I can't answer that, can I?" Icarus responded. His brow raised again, ever so slightly, but something about the movement, however small, irked me. It was a challenge, and I didn't like backing down from challenges.

But I also knew better.

I pressed my lips together for a moment as I looked the rest of him over, considering.

"Does the queen know, you think?" I asked, instead of answering him. "Does she know her court has access to the old glamour?"

"The real question," Icarus said, "is why does it matter? You see ..." he set down the scroll he'd been reading, unnoticed to me before, and started a slow sideways step around the room, almost as if he was beginning to circle me. "Even if they do, even if the queen has figured it out and planned to build herself a little army of these new-glamour wielding fae, she's facing the same problem I am."

He stopped moving, this time sizing me up instead.

"And what is that?" I asked.

"You," he said, simply. "The fact that you exist. One word from you, and anything any one of us truly tries to do against you … it's undone. Surely, Aurra, you've realized that by now."

I knew, at least, that it was part of the reason I still stood. The queen had seen me pull magic from a place I shouldn't have been able to, called forth the wells of my glamour even when they were run dry. I'd thought she was compelled by duty, at least a little.

It hadn't occurred to me that she was compelled, instead, entirely by fear.

"Why are you even telling me this?" I asked, all of a sudden. "Doesn't it work to your advantage to lie to me?"

Icarus shrugged. "I've always promised to be honest to you where no one else would."

Honest.

That wasn't exactly the word I'd use to describe this towering, horned, black-winged fae of the forbidden wilds.

Gorgeous. Deceptive. Cruel.

Those were better words.

I focused on the last two and forced out a half bark of a laugh, even though my mind wanted to linger on the way the shadows cast by the fire now at his back only served to make him glow with his uniquely dark beauty.

"Honest? You? What makes you think I'd believe anything you're telling me—now or ever?"

"I'm not asking you to have faith in me," Icarus said. "I'm asking you to have faith in yourself."

My lips parted, but I had nothing to say to that. Before I had to, however, Icarus held out his hands.

"Command me to tell the truth, Aurra. Use your power on me."

"I—"

I stumbled over my words as my mind struggled to catch up. I suddenly found myself breathless, a deep pit settling in my stomach as the image played itself out in my mind, of me commanding Icarus to do … well … *anything.* I already hated that I'd used my powers on other fae, even when I'd done it on accident. That was bad enough, but to do it to Icarus?

Something about that seemed so fundamentally wrong that it physically sickened me.

The wringing in my stomach didn't stop rage from flaring up in me too, however, when I saw the amusement play across the dark fae's face.

"Come now, please tell me you're not afraid to use the Tongues."

I blurted out my answer too quick. "I'm not afraid." I said, inwardly flinching at how clearly I was lying. Icarus didn't need to use his glamour on me to make my truth so painfully obvious.

"What are you then?"

Had Icarus moved closer, or had I?

We were standing almost close enough to touch now, but I didn't dare tear my eyes away to see for sure. It didn't matter. All that mattered was the way my breath suddenly hitched, and from the way his chest rose beneath the dark curls that spilled over his shoulders, so had his.

*What are you then?*

I didn't know the answer to Icarus' question. I had an idea of why the idea sickened me in a general sense, why it felt so wrong to force other fae—and humans, too—to do my bidding. But that wasn't the reason I found myself so averse to following his suggestion.

It was because I didn't want to force *him.*

It was foolish, the very idea of it. Icarus had tried to force me, had tried to manipulate me through omission—another kind of lie as cruel, or maybe even more cruel than an outright one—into doing his dark work. So why, then, was it not only impossible for me to use my power to get the answers I needed, but even more impossible for me to tell him why that was.

I could have floundered there for hours, drowning slowly, but Icarus put me out of my misery.

"I *want* you to command me, Aurra," he said, his voice lower, softer now. One of us stepped closer, but again, I was lost too deep in his eyes to know which one it was. Perhaps it was both of us. I couldn't feel my physical body anymore. I didn't exist, nothing did, nothing outside of the dark pools of Icarus' eyes as they held mine, and his voice as it wrapped around me, each one sweeter and more dangerous than the last. "I'm asking you to do this for me, *for me,* Aurra. My Storm …" His breath caught for a moment. "Can you do that for me?"

This time when my lips parted and a sigh slipped from between them, it wasn't in exasperation or anger, it was frustration.

"I don't have much glamour yet. I don't want to waste it."

Somehow, we'd moved even closer. I could see the curl of

Icarus' lashes, see the individual hues in his dark eyes, see the slightest twitch at the outer corner of his mouth as he reached out to me and took my hands.

"Then let me give you mine."

Before I had the chance to respond, I felt it. I felt *him*.

The magic flowed from Icarus into me, searing through my veins like fire. It was a powerful, all-consuming sensation that left me gasping for breath. I could feel his glamour taking hold, amplifying my own power and making me feel as though I could conquer the world.

But it was more than just power. It was Icarus himself, his essence and his energy flowing through me. It was an intimate connection that left me feeling vulnerable and exposed, yet at the same time, exhilarated.

I looked up at him, my eyes wide and trembling, and saw the same raw intensity reflected back at me.

I gasped again, my voice as raw as I felt inside. "I didn't know you could do that."

"Normally, a fae couldn't. Not unless they were in your court. Not unless you had the same glamour."

I reached out and flexed my fingers as inside, I reached for my glamour. I found only the new glamour, but it now ran inside the veins that I'd thought were only reserved for the one I'd inherited.

"But I think you've learned by now that I'm not just any fae."

My eyes widened and something like excitement welled up inside me, the endless possibilities that this presented dying the moment my gaze landed on the blackening tips of Icarus' fingers. He tried to draw them back, to hide them from me, but he was too late.

So, instead, he leaned in closer, his lips brushing against my ear as he whispered, "Now, My Storm. Command me."

My mind was a jumbled mess of desire and fear, but I knew what I had to do. I closed my eyes and focused, drawing on the newfound power within me. And then, in a voice that shook with emotion, I spoke the words that would bind Icarus to the truth.

"From this moment forward, Icarus, Lord of the Wildness, you will tell me no lies. You will speak nothing to me but the truth, keeping no secrets, until the moment that door behind me opens and we are no longer alone, you and I."

I was careful to speak the command so that it bound us only together for now, for this specific moment. He'd given me his trust, and I wanted to repay him in kind. It felt better that way.

This time, when I commanded the fae, I didn't feel guilt.

I felt, instead, a thrill, a tingle as I felt the glamour take hold of Icarus and saw the slight shudder that wracked his body as he registered it.

And I registered it, too.

For the first time since I'd met Icarus, since I'd met *any* of the fae who'd lorded over me, controlled me, or tried to gain some advantage from me, I was the one in control. I shouldn't have enjoyed the feeling, I tried to deny, even to myself, that I enjoyed the feeling.

But I did.

It excited me in a way that terrified me more than anything.

*This was what it truly felt like to wield the throne's power.*

# CHAPTER NINE

"Now, Aurra. You know fate won't leave us alone for long."

I opened my eyes and met his gaze once more, feeling the weight of his words. He was right, of course. Fate had a way of meddling in my affairs, twisting and turning until everything was once again upended, leaving chaos in its wake. And I knew that our time together, alone and bound by truth, was already quickly running out.

I wanted to savor this moment, this feeling of power and control. I wanted to explore this newfound part of myself, but I couldn't waste the opportunity that had been handed right to me. So, as much as I wanted to give into this moment, to surrender to this feeling, I instead closed my eyes to focus, took a steadying breath, and asked the one thing I so most desperately needed to know.

"What is your plan in all this, really?" I asked. "Not some small part of it. All of it. Your grand scheme, the end you wish to accomplish."

When I opened my eyes again, it was to find Icarus

looking at me with a mix of awe and—dare I even think it—reverence. It was a look I'd never seen before on him, certainly never directed at me. It made my heart race and my stomach flutter in a way that made my skin flush with heat.

"You're incredible," Icarus said, his voice barely above a whisper. "So much stronger than you realize."

I felt that warmth spread further through me at his words. "I don't feel strong," I admitted.

"That's because you've never had the chance to truly use your power. But now …" He trailed off, his eyes darkening with a hunger that matched my own.

"Now what?" I asked, taking a step closer to him.

"Now we have the chance to do something great," he said, his voice low and seductive. "You asked me what my grand plans are? What I aim to accomplish at the end of all this?"

I nodded, my breath catching slightly as I looked into those dark eyes of his widening slightly as he stared off through me for a moment, to something only he could see.

"Would you believe me if I told you it was to change the faerie courts of Luxia, to make it better for all of us."

Now I understood why he'd demanded I glamour him. If it weren't for the bonds of the glamour I still felt stretching so taut between us, I wouldn't have believed him. Not for a second.

Even with the glamour, I was struggling.

"How?" I asked. "And … why? I thought you wanted power."

"Of course I do," he said. "And that's why, to fix it, I'm going to take the throne and end the rule of the tyrannical Eastern Court for good."

At least that answer, I believed.

"And how do you plan to do that?"

His eyes focused in on me for a moment. "By ridding this kingdom of all four courts. It's one kingdom. We should be united."

I swallowed hard, trying to process the weight of his words. He wanted to rid Luxia of its courts? He was bound to tell the truth, but it sounded like he was lying to himself more than anything. What would ridding the kingdom of the courts do except give whoever still ruled over it absolute power?

*Oh.*

"My court is the perfect example for why you shouldn't be divided," Icarus continued, as understanding dawned on me. "All the houses should be abolished and the fae, and our powers, intermingle. The death of the king and the return of the glamour was a sign that the old rein has ended, and it's time a new one began. We'll be stronger this way."

My lips parted, but I struggled to find an answer to what he said.

Not because I didn't believe him, but because I did. I almost believed *in* him.

*Almost.*

"And my part in this?"

His face softened slightly as his eyes once more shifted to see me, and not the invisible dream beyond. "It was always just as I told you," he said. "I'd hoped to teach you the ways of the new glamour before it was too late. Before you took up the mantle of your father, and in doing so ..."

He trailed off, and for the first time, I saw a slight flicker of a struggle in his eyes.

But whatever he'd been trying to keep from me, it

tumbled out of him, prodded by the glamour that had wrapped around his tongue.

"In doing so, you made yourself my enemy."

*You made yourself my enemy.*

"I'm sorry, My Storm, but there's no place for you in my new reality. Not as queen, the other courts wouldn't stand for that."

"No one else will bow to you, Icarus," I said. "I've seen how the other fae fear you."

*How they hate you.*

That, at least, I kept to myself. Unlike Icarus, I was not bound by the glamour to speak the whole truth as it came to my mind. Not that I needed to. From the way Icarus' eyes darkened, he'd inferred it on his own.

"They do fear me," he said, "but they fear their Lords and Ladies, more. If faced with a choice, with *my* choice I intend to offer them, they will choose to follow me. I'm sure of it."

"And how are you so sure?"

The questions came too easily, now. Some of the charm had started to wear off. I felt less like I was seeking answers, and more and more like I was leading an interrogation.

Some of that heat that had flooded between us earlier had begun to cool off. It was slowly dawning on me what Icarus was truly saying, what he intended to do, and what that might mean for me—let alone all of Luxia, the kingdom I'd only recently began to discover my responsibility to take care of.

"Because commoners, human and fae, do love an underdog—especially once I reveal the deep corruption at the heart of this kingdom, we'll see who's side they take in the war."

"The war?"

"You heard the Oracle speak. You saw the vision, as did I," he continued. "It doesn't matter which one. One thing is true of any kingdom, war is always on their doorstep if they know where to look for it."

I felt myself step back from him before I realized I was doing it.

"Speak plainly, Icarus."

"I thought I already was."

"Speak plainly—" I reiterated, "so *I* think you are."

A slight smile pulled once more at the corner of Icarus' mouth. He dipped his head slightly, advancing one of his own steps forward with each one of my own that I took back.

He was upon me in an instant, his stride so far outpacing my own.

"I'm here to start a war, My Storm. Either *before* the queen learns to equip her court, or after I'm able to weaponise them myself."

That image, the bodies and the red, red sun, forced itself to the surface of my memory once more, as it had all too often since the moment I first saw it. That image, the bodies and the red, red sun, forced itself to the surface of my memory once more, as it had all too often since the moment I first saw it. I swallowed hard, trying to shake the image away, but it was no use. It had already taken root in my mind, more real than ever before. I could feel it growing around me, turning from a vision into something more. Something imminent. Something all too real.

I felt the heat of that red sun. I heard the screams of the dying, the crushing, crunching weight of bodies bearing down on one another as they piled higher and higher. The stench of war, of blood and iron and sweat filled my nostrils, threatening to overwhelm me.

I took one last step back, trying once again to shake this thing that had taken hold of me, but misjudged my own weight. Before I even knew I was falling, Icarus' hands were upon me, reaching out to catch me with a firm grip on my upper arms. Though I couldn't feel his skin on mine, the fabric wasn't enough to keep me from feeling that ever-preset bond that had stretched between me and him from the moment we met.

As I stared up into Icarus' eyes, the image of that vision, of the prophecy the Oracle had spoken over me, over both of us, it flickered and faded away. All I saw, in that moment, was him.

Icarus.

The Dark Fae.

My enemy.

But I didn't see my enemy. I didn't see the rogue, villainous fae of the Wildness that I'd been warned of time and time again, even by himself. All I saw was that strange, beautiful creature that had rescued me from his own Wildness that first day when I first faced the fae and knew them to be real.

"Why are you doing this?" The fear was gone from my voice when I asked it, but there was a new weight that hadn't been there before. "Why are you doing this to us?"

"Because," he said, his own voice so soft, so sweet, not the voice of a monster that had just admitted that his grand plan was to start the bloodshed I'd so feared, "it has to be done."

My brow furrowed. "Just because that's your truth doesn't mean that's *the* truth."

For a second, Icarus mulled on his. His arms were still around me, my body only held up by his own strength.

"You can't stop fate, My Storm."

He was no longer talking about visions or prophesies. My heart raced with a forbidden excitement that I couldn't deny. I looked into his eyes, and I saw something in them that made my heart race. It was a look of desire, of need. He leaned down, his lips only inches from mine, and whispered, "And fate brought us together for a reason."

But even as we were so close to once again giving in to our desires, I couldn't shake the feeling that something was coming, something that would change everything.

My breath hitched, and before he could lean in closer, close that gap as we already had one too many times, I had to ask one thing more.

"Why did you bring my sister here, Icarus?"

His grip on me tightened slightly. "For you."

"You brought her here to antagonize me?"

"I brought her here to make sure you couldn't drive me away."

It was a fair enough answer. But I needed more.

"But as your fiancé?"

His answer was quick and sharp. "As her protector."

*That* caught me off guard.

"You think I could bring a human here under any other circumstance and have a single fae care whether she lived or died?" he asked, only further serving to muddle the image that had been forming so clear in my mind. "You think she would be safe, anywhere, even with me—unless everyone around me thought that I cared about her enough to make them fear touching her?"

It was a fair answer. Too fair.

So I asked, plainly, what really concerned me.

"But do you love her?"

The arms holding mine went rigid. He hesitated, and that meant everything.

"Do you love my sister, your betrothed?" I asked again, and with the second question, his hesitation only grew more obvious.

I saw the way he fought whatever word was trying to force its way off his tongue.

Before he could answer me, however, that thing I'd felt approaching was suddenly upon us. In the silence of his struggle, I heard the footsteps on the other side of the door too late—and when the door finally opened, shattering the moment and bringing us back to reality, I knew that Icarus' earlier premonition had been right.

Fate had arrived, and there was no escaping its grasp.

Ada, my sister, stood in the door just as Icarus finally gave me my answer.

"No."

But it was too late. I'd felt the bond of my glamour break before the word was spoken, and I knew it for what it was.

I knew what that meant.

I knew why he struggled.

And that was why I fled.

# CHAPTER TEN

*HE LOVED HER.*

Ada might not know I was once her sister, but if she hadn't viewed me as an enemy before, she had to now. I'd seen the look on her face when she saw me and Icarus together. I'd been found in far more compromising positions with Icarus before, but this time felt different.

This time felt so much worse.

It didn't matter that this time I was fully clothed, not when our intentions, that heat between us that radiated like the Midsommar sun, were all too obvious.

Even knowing that, feeling that shame and frustration and disappointment, and the betrayal of my sister was still not the thought that repeated itself over and over inside the darkest, echoing corners of my brain.

*He loved her.*

Icarus, the dark fae, loved my sister, Ada.

No bond between us, fate or otherwise, could trump that.

I felt hollow, emptied out, desperate. But more than that, I felt alone.

So, I fled towards the one place I still felt safe, the one place I knew I should have gone straight away. I never should have gone to Icarus. He'd left me only more confused, more muddled, my thoughts wound so tight that it was hard to see where one ended and the next began.

I ran through the castle, ignoring the guards and courtiers that shot me strange looks. I was too focused on getting to Shiel's rooms, too determined not to let the chorus of voices in my head get to me, first. There was no bond between me and Shiel that could lead me to him, not like the one that had taken me so easily to the dark fae's side.

Knowing that only served to humiliate me further.

My feet led me down winding corridors and up staircases until finally I found myself outside his door. It took me too long to get there, too long to follow the trail of whispers and wrong turns until I finally succumbed to demanding directions from a guard.

Guilt refused to let me use my powers, so I had to hope he didn't tell anyone what I'd asked.

I was supposed to be studying still, after all.

But I couldn't go back to my lessons, not now. Not while the image of my sister's shocked face was still burned into the back of my eyelids, even as Icarus' touch still burned on my skin.

This time, I hesitated before bursting inside the room. I'd wanted to catch Icarus by surprise, hoped to find him doing something that perhaps he shouldn't, but Shiel didn't deserve that. I deserved that, and that was just what I'd gotten.

I cringed, waiting for a beat before I allowed myself to knock, until the pain of that mental reminder faded enough for me to hide it from my face, even if there was no hiding what had just happened between Icarus and I from myself.

Shiel's voice called out, bidding me enter, and I shoved my way inside with a desperation that somehow only managed to knock a couple of books off a shelf placed a little too close to where the door swung open.

I was already gathering these up, glad for the excuse for why my face had turned so red, by the time Shiel looked up from where he scribbled at a desk strewn with papers the way his sick bed once had been.

His own voice was breathless when he saw me. "What is it, Aurra? Are you alright?"

Of course, I wasn't alright. Now that I was here, however, I didn't know how to answer.

What did I want from Shiel, really?

I wasn't sure. I came here on instinct. That was all I knew.

"I—I'm fine. I just had a break in my lessons, so I wanted to see you. I haven't so much as seen you, Zev, or Finch all week. I had some … thoughts … I wanted to run by you."

He stopped in his tracks, and for a moment, I saw him struggle between the paper still grasped between his fingers, and me.

"It's fine, Shiel," I said, my own steps slowing. "It's not urgent. You can finish what you're doing, first."

For a second, he struggled still, but then he just nodded at me, glanced once at the door to make sure it was shut, and then stepped back to where his pen had been abandoned and returned to his hasty scribbling with a furrowed brow.

I, meanwhile, was too relieved for a moment longer to gather myself to feel jilted.

Something about Shiel's presence, or perhaps the warm

western light that cast all the room in a golden glow, had begun to settle the pounding of my heart. It was hardly the warm welcome I might have wanted, but it was always this way with Shiel. He was hot and cold, it was his nature. It was better not to dwell on it, better to just hope he warmed again on his own once he'd had time to finish whatever task it was he was so hell-bent on accomplishing.

He was a single-minded fae. Sometimes, it worked to my advantage.

Others, it left me scuffling my feet as I wondered what to do with my own wandering mind.

Shiel had been given a suite far smaller than mine, or even Icarus', small enough that if I were him, Lord of the Western Court, I'd have been offended.

Maybe he was offended, maybe that was why his desk and floor were littered with papers only loosely bundled into piles that may or may not at some point be sent back to his advisors on raven wing. Or, maybe they were just more drafts like the one that had nearly driven us apart not so long ago, remnants of a mind that seemed always so torn between one thing and another.

This was the same kind of madness.

Shiel had multiple tables pulled together to make one large one and across all of it were different parchments, scrolls, books, and inkwells. He stood in the midst of all these papers, his hair unruly, matching his rumpled clothes. Dark circle had taken up residence beneath his eyes, all too telling.

"You look awful. Have you slept at all?"

His eyes slowly raised from the scroll he'd been scribbling on to look up at me before they fell back down on the parchment.

"You're not the only one who's been keeping busy. Believe it or not," he said, "it's not easy to keep an entire court in line when you haven't so much as stepped foot in it for months."

A slight pang of guilt settled into the pit of my stomach, but it didn't last long, not when it was swallowed by the enormity of the rest that had already settled there. Just because Shiel had promised he would give up his court, in the end, if he needed to—if that was what it would take to see me seated on the Eastern Throne—didn't mean I wanted him to have to do it.

And from the looks of the fervor with which he was trying to keep up, he wasn't willing to give it up without a fight.

A proper fight.

*But would he go so far as Icarus was willing to?*

I couldn't think about what Icarus had told me, what he'd revealed under the influence of my glamour, without thinking about what had happened after—so I forced it from my mind before it could consume me again. Shiel had gone back to writing, his face intent as he was lost in thought. I watched him in silence, taking in the shape of him outlined against that afternoon sun.

I moved towards Shiel, careful not to step on any of the papers that had fallen onto the floor. I grabbed a chair from his bedside and pulled it over to the table and took a seat, resting my head in my hands as I looked up at him, still completely oblivious to me.

As I sat there, watching him work, I couldn't help but admire the way his eyes crinkled at the corners when he was deep in thought or the way his pen moved effortlessly across the paper. I'd never asked Shiel how he felt about his role as Lord. He always seemed to fit into that role so effortlessly, but here, in the quiet with him, it was anything but effortless. His work was tireless, and though it didn't exactly look like he *enjoyed* it, he seemed suited for it.

I'd learned a few things in my lessons.

I knew that though fae healed quickly, they only lived a little longer than humans. They kept to themselves for the most part. The only court where humans and fae resided together was here, in the Eastern Court. It was the court that we first conquered when we arrived on these shores. The rest we built ourselves.

*Ourselves.*

Not for the first time since arriving here in the Eastern Court, I marveled a little at how quickly I'd switched sides. All my life I'd believed myself a human, bound myself to their stories, their traditions, and their beliefs. But it had only taken a couple of months for that to shift.

It mightn't have been so easy if my experience with humans had been anything other than wretched.

I forced my thoughts away from that past, so recent, still, but already feeling like it was an entire lifetime ago. There was no point in being bitter. I was safe now. My sister was, if not safe, at least *away* from that same past that had threatened to destroy us both, eventually. She'd never faced the same abuse that I had, but her life hadn't been a happy one. I'd tried to shield her, but in the end, she suffered right beside me.

And now, she suffered still, because of me.

I felt those dark thoughts rise up in me again, the ones that I was trying so desperately to run from, and felt myself reaching out for something, anything, to distract myself again. I found it this time in the distant sound of clanging steel coming from somewhere far down below in the courtyard.

I made my way over to the window and looked out at the courtyard below while Shiel continued to work, unbothered. I probably could have hurled a book—or even myself—from that window, and he wouldn't have even noticed.

A few of the guards were on their break and had congregated into a rough circle around a pair that were sparring in the middle. As I peered closer, I noticed Zev among them. What was Zev doing, training with the guard? Was that how he'd chosen to occupy his time? Was that what he'd been ordered to do? And Finch?

I'd been surprised he hadn't found a way to see me. He'd tried so desperately in the past. Perhaps he was being kept as busy as I was, assigned his own tasks meant to keep him from making any trouble. If the queen hadn't, it wouldn't have surprised me if Shiel had stepped in and done it himself.

Down below, most of Zev's clothes had been cast aside to give him mobility, so he was left wearing only his trousers. He wielded a sword with an easy grace, backpedaling on nimble feet while exchanging lightning-fast strikes with his opponent. Sweat coated his chest and glistened under the sun, but it wasn't his incredible physique that caught my breath.

Even from so high up, I could make out the smooth, unmarked surface of his skin.

His tattoos. They were gone.

A deep stabbing pain dug between my ribs.

That did explain why he hadn't come looking for me the moment I was left alone with Icarus this time. He hadn't been able to feel the beating of my own heart beside his own.

That realization stung like salt poured into an open wound. It cut into me, bruised me, left me bleeding.

But it was my own fault. I'd been so wrapped up in my studies, so consumed with trying to prove to my mother that I could fall into line and earn my place on the throne, that I'd neglected the fae who'd brought me here to begin with.

The fae that I'd come to know as my family, the ones that actually wanted me. In doing so, even in that short period of time, I'd already lost something.

That stabbing pain deepened, turning into a throb that refused to go away. It was a buoy, the harder I tried to push it down, the faster and higher it rose as soon as I let go. It clouded every other thought from my mind, darkening the outer corners of my vision as I peered down at Zev below in the courtyard, until all I could see was the distant golden glow of his unmarked skin.

What a mess I'd made.

How long ago was it that Shiel had come for me? How long since he'd told me his suspicions, since he'd dragged me from an old life that felt so hazy now.

Not long enough, not enough for me to have entangled this new life so thoroughly that I couldn't see my own way out of it. I was both the spider and the web, both the predator and my own prey.

That stabbing pain grew and deepened and grew and deepened until it was a gnawing chasm inside me. It spread outward, taking hold of my body, wrapping tight, grimy fingers around my throat until it threatened to choke me. I fought against it, but the harder I resisted, the tighter it squeezed, the more it burned and spread until my vision blurred with the hot sting of tears.

I was drowning, and not for the first time.

But this time, try as I could to swim, I only sank deeper.

I would have continued to sink, to flounder and flail into the depths of this mess I'd made for myself, if it weren't for the voice that reached out for me, offering a way out of the dark, a hand to lift me from the darkness.

"Aurra?"

It still took me a moment for the voice to register, and then a moment longer for the dark corners of my vision to recede even as I turned to face the fae now looking up at me, concern deepening the line between his brows.

Shiel's hair had grown considerably longer in the months since we first locked eyes that fateful day at the market. The sun kissed curls fell over his forehead, just too short for the wayward locks to be tucked behind his ears. I couldn't remember the last time I'd looked at Shiel, *really* looked at him, not like this—not with the reflected light of the western sun illuminating him with a halo of golden light so that he seemed to glow from somewhere within.

He wore only soft leather breeches and a white linen shirt with the sleeves rolled up past the rounded muscle of his forearms, now frozen halfway through reaching for another stack of yet-unwritten letters. He was ink smudged and wrinkled, the buttons of his shirt done too hastily, and still, despite all that, he looked as regal as he had the day we met. More, even, now that I knew him for who he was. For what he was.

"Aurra ... are you alright?"

Shiel's voice once again pierced through the fog that had enveloped my mind.

This time when he asked the question, there was none of the annoyance that had tinged his voice earlier. Again, however, when I tried to respond to him, I found the answer catching in my throat.

Alright?

I was far from it, far from anything other than even vaguely resembled *alright.*

But as I looked into the concerned eyes of the fae before me, I felt a warmth spread through my chest, melting away some of the cold that had taken root there. It was as if his very presence had the power to soothe me, to calm the raging storm inside of me.

Not entirely, but enough to loosen the knot that had formed so solidly at the back of my throat.

"I don't know," I finally managed to choke out. "I feel like … like I've lost something."

It was worse than that, really, but I didn't know how to tell him. How was I supposed to say that what I'd lost was only the beginning, that I felt like whatever that was, whatever it was I was losing, I was just going to keep losing parts of it, parts of me, until there was nothing left.

I couldn't say it, but it seemed I didn't have to.

Shiel's expression softened further as he set the stack of letters down on the table beside him and stood, his eyes never leaving mine. He crossed the room to me in a few quick strides, taking my hand in his. The moment our skin touched, something fluttered back to life deep inside me.

His hands were rough, too rough, the kind of rough that made mine feel soft. As if on instinct, as if reading my thoughts, Shiel turned my hands over, both our eyes dropping to examine the soft, smooth skin of my palms. Once, not too long ago, these hands of mine were scarred and calloused from years working at my parent's mill. I'd thought nothing of it, like the rest of my lot in life, hands as hard and cracked as untreated leather were just another facet of the life I'd been dealt. Compared to the cruelties of the rest of it, callouses and cracks were a kindness.

But now my hands were as smooth and soft as silk, the skin so new and untouched that the palms hardly creased. The magic my mother had used to hide me, to disguise my powers and my position, had protected me, too.

I started to pull away, but Shiel's hands tightened over mine. His eyes drew my back up to look at him, and in them I saw a spark I'd almost forgotten once existed between us. This fae, this Lord of the Western Court, had spent so long trying to protect me, not just from the evils of this world, but from myself.

This was the fae that had rescued me from my father's lashings, that man's hand on me the last thing I was sure to ever see if he hadn't.

This was the fae that had saved me from the vile man my parents had betrothed me to, who had even then followed my wishes and still somehow dealt that monster a fate like no other, one only befitting a man who'd murdered his previous wives and seemed determined to do the same to me.

This was the fae that had saved me from Icarus.

Icarus.

A deep, core-shaking shudder rumbled up through me.

I'd been blinded by that dark fae from the very beginning, but it wasn't Icarus who first dragged me into the world of the fae, into my destiny.

It was Shiel. This golden-haired creature before me with eyes as bright and blinding as the setting sun itself, this was the fae, the male, the man who—despite a stubbornness even greater than my own—had held me all night in that tent after he'd torn my betrothal papers to shreds. The same one that swore his allegiance to me even if it cost him the court he so desperately tried now to save. This was the fae that had brought himself to the brink of death for me time and time again.

Not Icarus.

It wasn't until I felt the soft scratch of Shiel's stubble beneath my fingers that I realized what I was doing. I cupped the side of the fae lord's face in one hand, his own still cradling mine, our bodies now a hair's breadth away from each other since I'd stepped up closer to reach him.

Not for the first time, something bloomed within me. Between us.

More than bloomed. This thing, it had been growing, unfurling, blossoming for months, from the moment I laid eyes on this glittering gold fae. Even in the weeks we were apart, even in the moments when hate and anger were the only feelings the sight of him dragged up in me, this thing had been steadily strengthening.

"My dearest Aurra ..." Shiel whispered. "It's okay to lose things. Losing something doesn't have to mean it's lost forever. It just means you have to find it again."

He pulled my hand away from his face only so he could press his lips too softly to my knuckles. "Whatever it is you think you've lost, let me help you find it."

# CHAPTER ELEVEN

THERE, BENEATH THE WEIGHT OF SHIEL'S GAZE, I DIDN'T FEEL SO lost anymore.

Once again, he'd found me, but this time ... this time, I wasn't going to let him go.

And apparently, from the way his gaze suddenly sharpened, neither was he. Something in him shifted, transformed as he read the change in me, too. His fingers unlaced from mine only so they could find my waist instead. I'd seen him this focused before, but never on me. He looked at me with an intensity usually reserved for his work, for keeping his own court in line. Now, with his hands tightening around me, pulling me closer, his eyes locked with mine and didn't waver.

"I'm sorry."

His apology caught me off guard.

"I should have known you needed me when you came. I think I did, I just ..." He trailed off slightly, any excuse he might have made trailing off with it. "I like to think I know you well enough by now to know when you need me."

"It's only been a few months."

"It feels longer than that." Shiel stopped and cocked his head to the side slightly. "No, not longer. Just … just different."

For one, brief moment, his eyes did leave mine, but only so they could trace the lines of my face, slowly, as if he was carefully memorizing me.

"It's strange to think there was a day before fate brought us together in that marketplace."

*Fate, yet again.*

Icarus had once spoken of fate. No, more than once.

If it weren't for everything that had unfolded since he first spoke words of destiny into my life, I still wouldn't believe in fate. But now … standing here, waiting to take my throne, with the seed of a powerful glamour running through my veins and the weight of an age-old prophecy spoken over me, I'd be a fool *not* to at least entertain a belief in fate.

Or, at the very least, some version of it that had been seemingly driving me ever closer and closer towards a point that felt like whatever it had in store for me was now looming just out of sight.

Not that I could have seen it if I tried, not now, not with the way Shiel's touch had begun to make everything else start to fade away. My heart had steadied, if only so that I could feel it quicken at the slightest shift of the lord's touch on my skin.

"You really think it was fate?"

My question came out as a whisper, almost inaudible, as if I was afraid to ask. As if I was afraid to hear an echo of the dark fae's words again. Or, perhaps, I was afraid because I wanted to hear that echo. I wanted to believe that fate wasn't as cruel as I'd begun to fear.

"Fate? Luck?" Shiel stopped and shook his head. "They're one and the same. At least, as far as I'm concerned."

"Luck?" I asked. "Have you seen where we are, what's happening around us? You call that luck?"

The words were meant half in jest, but there was too much truth to them.

That was why I was so surprised by Shiel's answer again. It came quick, without thought.

"I'm here with you. Any fae who wouldn't count that as luck is a fool."

I couldn't help the slight smile that pulled at the outer corner of my mouth.

"What?" Shiel asked, his own brows furrowing. "You think I'm lying?"

"I think you're reaching."

That frown only deepened, as did the firmness of his grip on my waist. "I'm dead serious, Aurra," he said. "I know there's a lot going on, there's so much in the balance—not just for you, for both of us—but there's no place I'd rather be right now than here, by your side."

A slight sigh whistled between his lips as, for just a moment, that hardened mask of his slipped for a moment. His face softened with something like regret, the furrowed brows turning up slightly in the center as he tried to read deeper the expression on my own face.

"I should have listened to you the moment you came to me," he said, his voice soft and full of all the feeling he'd briefly let show on his face—already fleeting. "I'm an idiot, you know. When it comes to … to these kinds of things. I'm not used to them."

"These kinds of things?" I asked the question, if only to try to stop my heart from skipping the way it did when he said it. I knew what he meant. I mostly knew. But I needed to hear it from him, and in no uncertain terms. I couldn't handle another crushing embarrassment, I couldn't handle the shame that would follow if I was wrong—not after the embarrassment and shame that still clung to me.

Shiel wrapped his hands a little tighter again, so tight it was almost enough to stop me from drawing breath.

"I can't get close enough to you, Aurra," Shiel whispered. "I have to stop myself from hurting you, even now, just because I wish I could simply pull you into myself—where I can protect you, always."

"Protect me?"

"And love you."

His answer came so quick this time, so without hesitation, that it actually *did* stop me from drawing breath. For several beats, I looked up into those golden glowing eyes and searched them for the truth that glimmered back at me as plain as day. I didn't need an enchantment to know that Shiel was telling me the truth.

He meant what he said.

Every golden, radiating, heat-inducing syllable of it.

It was almost painful to force myself to draw that breath I'd held, if only because it meant I had to find my own words to answer him.

"Love?"

The word sounded like a swear, the way it clawed and scratched its way up the back of my throat, like it was vomited instead of spoken. I didn't know the last time I'd used that word. Didn't know if I ever had. It had certainly, *certainly* never been spoken to me. Not even at me, *about* me.

The outer corners of Shiel's eyes crinkled ever so slightly, the mere sight of those soft lines sending my heart skipping so violently that my head began to spin.

"Surely, you didn't think I was willing to give up everything, to lay down my court, my own crown, my little kingdom, for a future queen out of mere *duty?*" he asked. There was no condescension in his tone, only the slightest amusement. It was so foreign a sound on him, so opposite of his usual cool, calm, seriousness, that it was almost too much to comprehend. I looked up into those shining eyes flickering between mine, at the laugh building at their outer corners but not yet spilling over onto his tongue, and I felt something start to melt deep within me. "Aurra ..."

His voice trailed off as one hand removed itself from my waist so he could brush back the tangled red locks that now fell along either side of my face.

For the briefest second, his eyes once again left mine to search that face, and a strange look overtook him.

That melting sensation in my stopped, hardened almost as soon as it had begun.

"What is it?" I asked, tense as the muscles that had seized deep within me.

For a second, Shiel's mouth hung open before he found his own words. "Sometimes," he admitted, "I miss the face of the girl I rescued from that mill."

His words shocked me. Not because they were so unexpected, but because I felt it, too.

I'd yet to grow used to the face looking back at me in the

mirror.

I started to shrink back from him, only half-consciously. My eyes turned away, but as soon as they did, Shiel tightened his grip on me, once again taking hold of me with both arms, as if to keep me from pulling back anymore.

"You're beautiful, still, Aurra," Shiel gasped, the sound of it forcing my eyes back up to meet his. "I just … it wasn't this face that first drove me mad. It wasn't this face that first stole my heart."

I still felt myself instinctively pulling away, but Shiel didn't relent. He held me tight, lowering his face until it was closer to mine, before he continued, voice so soft it was barely above a whisper.

"But it wasn't your old face, either," he said. "It was you."

*You.*

Something about that one, simple word, it released the tension that had tried to pull me from him. I stopped drawing back, and instead fell into him, both of us closing that tiny gap that remained together until our lips crashed into each other, sealing our steadily shortening breaths with a kiss.

It wasn't the first time I'd kissed Shiel, but it might as well have been. Something about that moment when our lips met, trembling and hungry, was different—and it wasn't just because it was the first time I'd kissed him with my true form, with the lips that still felt new and foreign to me.

It was because this time, when we kissed, we didn't hold back.

Neither of us.

It was as if there was no tomorrow, no kingdom to rule,

and no expectations to meet. We were just two people, two fae, lost in the moment, lost in each other. Shiel's lips were fierce and demanding against mine, his hands gripping me tightly as he pulled me closer to him. I could feel his heat, his strength, his passion, burning through every pore of my being. His hands roamed over my body, tracing the curves and contours of my form as if he couldn't get enough of me. His touch was electric, sending shivers down my spine and into my core as his hands found my hair and dug into it, fisting at the curls at the nape of my neck until he dragged a soft moan from my parted lips.

I felt a smug smile pull at his lips as I panted, my own fingers tangling in his hair as I pulled him closer to me. His hardness pressed against me, drawing a gasp from my lips as I pulled away to look up into those golden eyes of his, now darkened with the same desire that sprang up within me.

It wasn't the first time I'd felt this heat, intense and deep, but this was the first time I let it consume me.

I drew my hands down to rest on Shiel's chest, feeling the hardness of his muscles beneath my fingers as I held that intensity of his gaze a moment longer.

"Take me."

Shiel didn't need to be asked twice. He lifted me up and carried me to the bed, laying me down gently as he began to undress me, his fingers fumbling with the ties on my dress.

As he pulled the fabric away, leaving nothing but the sheer soft silk of my shift between us, I felt a blush rise to my cheeks. But then he leaned down and kissed me again, and all my self-consciousness melted away. My hands tore at the hem of his shirt until together, we pulled it up over his head and tossed it aside. Then my hands were on his body, and his were tangled in the soft white silk of my shift and the long red tendrils of my hair. His hips pressed down into mine, grinding his arousal between my thighs.

Every other thought left my mind except for one.

I wanted him. I wanted him so badly that it hurt.

I wanted him so badly that a sigh tore its way out of my throat between our fevered kisses. He took my sigh as an invitation, his kisses growing even more heated until he was kissing his way down my neck, his lips trailing hot as coals over my skin. I gasped as he nipped at the sensitive spot just behind my ear, his hands moving down my body to my hips.

He stopped then, suddenly, lifting his hips slightly so that he hovered over me, his eyes burning with desire as he slowly, oh-so-slowly, took in the sight of me.

Only once his eyes had drank their fill did he begin to remove my shift next, too. I watched him through heavy-lidded eyes, my own desire building with each passing moment. When I was finally naked under him, he took a moment to simply look at me, his gaze roving over my body with a hunger that made me ache. Then he was on me again, his mouth finding mine as he began to explore my body with his hands and lips. I arched into him, my body craving more of his touch. Every nerve in my body was on fire, and I knew that I was lost to him.

One hand moved to his breeches, undoing to buttons so that the full length of him sprang forth. I felt the heat of his bare skin on mine as he pressed himself to the apex of my thighs. No sooner had our bodies brushed together then I felt myself blurt out.

"I've never done this before."

"Not even with—" He stopped, eying me for a moment with the question he nearly dared ask—but then didn't. I saw it flicker there, but it was gone just as quickly as it appeared.

He drew back just enough so that our bodies no longer touched, and I felt another rush of words tumble from my lips.

"I don't want you to stop," I breathed, desperation heavy on my tongue.

Shiel met my gaze.

"Then I'm not going to."

But his movements slowed, then. He leaned back, his eyes taking me in differently, now. He knelt above me as he slowly took off his breeches, one leg at a time, the muscled planes of his body somehow even more achingly beautiful with every agonizing moment that passed.

Frustration welled up in me, that ache in my body screaming, demanding to be satisfied. I squirmed beneath him, discomfort racing through me until I was unable to keep still, unable to keep from trying to pull him closer to me, *into* me. I reached for him, my hands trailing over the hardened abs of his stomach and then lower, but he drew back from my touch again, not enough to make me think he no longer wanted me, but enough to try and force me to slow, too.

He caught my hand, gently, and bent over so he could press my fingers to his lips in an even more agonizingly gentle kiss.

It was enough to draw another gasp, this one of exasperation, from my lips.

"I know how it's done," I started, even more desperate

now, my eyes cutting from his golden irises to the impossibly sexy body hovering too close and still too far above mine. "I was practically raised on a farm."

"We're not animals on a farm, Aurra," Shiel whispered, cutting me off. "Or, at least, not all of us are."

His eyes softened at the sight of my discomfort.

"Let me make this memorable for you, Aurra," he said. "And not in the way first times always are, but because I made it that way."

Something about his words, or perhaps the softness in his eyes when he said it, finally calmed the nerves that left me shifting beneath him. Though that fire still burned between my thighs, that ache still throbbing hard as ever, the pain of it shifted into something more like anticipation as his lips once again dropped to kiss the place where my ribs met between my breasts.

His cock pressed to the inside of my thighs again, driving me wild with desire even as he only allowed it to brush against me, not even anywhere near *into* me. His lips planted hot kisses along my body slowly, slower even than before. He moved down, each kiss as tender as if he were worshipping me, and each one driving me wilder until I was sure I was going to lose my mind.

Finally, his lips settled over mine again, and when they did, I felt an intense heat as his hips shifted ever-so-slightly and finally, he was pushing himself against the entrance of my sex.

He stopped then, just for as long as it took for him to meet my eyes and demand, "Look into my eyes Aurra, and don't look away."

He held my gaze as slowly, oh-so-slowly, he finally pressed inside of me.

The pleasure that shot through my body was unlike anything I'd ever felt before. I gasped against his lips, my nails digging into his back as he stopped then, and we stayed like that, the intensity of his gaze never leaving mine as I adjusted to the girth of him, barely pressed inside my entrance.

I felt my body yearning for more, felt my hips pressing upwards, trying to push him deeper inside, but he resisted me, even as his breaths grew shorter and sweat began to bead along the line of his brow.

"Aurra," he whispered my name again with a groan, his gaze breaking only so long as it took to press another kiss to my lips, before he drew back and met it again. "You have no idea how hard it is to …" he stopped and swore as I pushed my hips up again, his body trembling and his eyes rolling back slightly as just a little more of him pushed inside me. "Fuck, Aurra. I can't. I'm sorry."

He grabbed my wrists and pulled them up above my head, pinning them there as he lost control, his hips thrusting forward with a feral grunt as he finally he entered me. Fully entered me. I gasped as his cock filled me, stretching me in one hard motion.

With every movement, I felt my pleasure grow. His thrusts were slow and controlled, but deep, and I felt myself reaching something I'd never known before, something that seemed to go beyond pleasure and into the realm of ecstasy.

My hips moved against him, urging him on, and he responded with a deep growl that only spurred me on further. I felt an orgasm building inside me, the sensations intensifying until I was no longer sure where I ended and he began.

His body pinned mine down, crushed me, overpowered me as he took his pleasure from me, too. His grunts grew more labored, his hands tightening their grip on mine as he pumped more furiously, driving the full length of himself in and out of me each time.

More moans, soft gasps half stained with pleasure, escaped my lips as his pace increased. He'd grown feral, almost, so much so that if his cock was not so slick with our shared arousal, he might have hurt me. But pain was the last thing on my mind as I felt the last of my control slipping away, felt the pleasure rising in me too much. Just then, his mouth found mine again, his tongue shoving between my lips in a desperate attempt to claim me even further as I felt the orgasm cresting. He pulled away again, just as I felt myself hit my peak, and I saw in his eyes that he was there, too.

He slammed into me one final time, his body tensing as the orgasm rocked through him and into me, and we both cried out as we spilled over together. Tears were streaming down my cheeks when he pulled himself from me, finally, and for a second, I saw the fear that the sight of them dragged up in him.

"I'm so sorry, Aurra, I meant to be gentle ..."

Before he could say anything more, however, I pulled him into a kiss, only breaking it when my panting breaths were ready to form words. Still, my voice shook nearly as much as the rest of my body when I spoke.

"You didn't hurt me," I reassured him. "You were right, Shiel. I'll never forget that."

Finally, he collapsed onto his side, pulling me up against him so that I was now sprawled across his chest. His breathing was still labored, his heart hammering beneath me, and I felt a warmth inside me that I hadn't felt before.

He held me close, his arms tight around me, and I swore I felt him trembling, too.

# CHAPTER TWELVE

I<small>T WAS ALMOST INSULTING THAT NO ONE CAME LOOKING FOR ME</small> in the hours I spent wrapped in Shiel's sheets.

I fell asleep in his arms over and over, my fluttering lashes opening to see his own unmoving features silhouetted in, first —the setting golden hues of the sun—and then later that silvery blue of the moon that filtered in once night had long since fallen. I tried to lay still because even the smallest shift in my weight had Shiel suddenly twitching to pull me closer. I was already wrapped tightly in his arms, protected in the warmth he'd trapped from that golden sun itself just so he could radiate it into me.

Shiel's room seemed different without the cast of that western light. *His* light.

The windows were still open, but without that golden glow or the clash of steel from down below, even the slightest sound outside in the courtyard seemed to echo eerily. I could almost imagine the distant echo of fiends far off, the memory of the chase that had led us here, to my court, not so distant to yet be forgotten. I was lucky that those beasts hadn't chosen to haunt my nightmares. Not so lucky, however, because the things that usually haunted that space between sleep and waking were even more nightmarish.

It was as I lay there in the early hours of the morning right before dawn struck, half entangled still in the arms of the Western Court lord and half entangled in his sheets, that I heard it.

It was so distant I didn't recognize it at first.

It was like the call of a siren, distant, beautiful, and impossible to ignore. The moment the first syllable rose from the silence, I froze, my entire body unable to so much as move a muscle as it was joined by another, and then another, growing louder until it wasn't just a string of syllables, untamed noises, but a voice.

The moment I registered it for what it was, I knew exactly *who* it was, too.

I was on my feet so quickly it was a small miracle I didn't trip over either of my entanglements. As fast as I was, however, by the time my face was pressed to the panes of glass, there wasn't so much as a shadow to signal my sister, Ada down below. Her voice, already distant, was quickly fading.

As was the one that accompanied it.

That voice was the one that made bile rise up at the back of my throat, because it sounded all too much like mine. Not the voice that I'd grown so used to hearing, but the one that now sounded like a stranger spoke for me each time I opened my mouth.

I leaned forward, prying the window open further so I could lean out into the cool, early morning air to try and listen, to catch even the slightest whisper of their actual words. It was to no avail. All I heard above the slowly fading drone of their voices was the scratch of my own nails upon the glass as my grip tightened in frustration.

Too tight, apparently.

Before I realized what was happening, a high-pitched sound shattered the night. It wasn't for a second, until one of the intricate panes of red and gold glass fell apart in my hands, leaving the tips of my fingers shredded by tiny lines of blood brough forth by the broken shards, that I realized what had happened.

Shiel sat up too suddenly, his hand reaching for the knife he'd cast aside earlier, only to come back from beneath the pillow empty. His hand searched the blankets frantically for only a second, for the few moments it took for his mind to register it was not only missing, but not needed. There was no enemy present, after all. Not a physical one, anyway.

"What's wrong?" he asked, his voice still raked with tired gravel as he reached for me, now, instead. His frown, already furrowed deep within his brows, deepened as he laid eyes on my hand still frozen in the now empty pane. "You're bleeding."

He started getting up from the bed, but I shook my head. It stilled him for a moment, but he seemed frozen, suspended between waking and sleeping where every decision weighed too heavily.

"I didn't think the glass would be so fragile," I said, almost absentmindedly. My eyes still scanned the dark court-yard below. The voices were gone entirely, but their memory haunted me more than any nightmare could.

"Why are you at the window?"

"I ..." I trailed off, shaking my head as if I could shake that echo from my memory.

"What is it, Aurra?"

Shiel's voice had softened, returned once again to something more like the one belonging to the fae who had taken me to this bed just a few hours ago. I caught his eye, not so bright without his golden setting sun, but still just as tender— and it softened me, too. I felt the tension in my shoulders ease, my hands unclenching from the windowpane so I could rejoin him on the edge of the bed.

"I thought I heard my sister," I admitted, realizing how silly I sounded.

"And that's a reason for all ... this?" Shiel's voice paused as he reached over to brush hair from my face. It was only then, as he peeled the strands from my sticky cheeks, that I realized I'd broken out in a cold sweat. I looked down at myself, at the pale skin lit by moonlight now glittering with tiny damning droplets.

My brows pulled together, my mind still knitting my thoughts together, half scattered by sleep and the other by the sound that had so shaken me.

I shook my head again, more slowly this time. "I thought I heard her talking to Fauna. To the changeling."

Shiel's face darkened slightly. "You think they're plotting something?"

That thought had occurred to me, yes. But I'd have been lying to Shiel if I told him that was what had bothered me about it so much. And right now, after everything, as I looked into his face so contorted with concern for me, I couldn't so much as stretch the truth.

"I was jealous, I think," I admitted. "That she could talk to someone who wears my face, when now I doubt she'll ever want to talk to me."

Shiel's eyes narrowed. Sleep must have finally drifted far enough away from him that he noticed even the subtlest slip in my voice.

"Now?"

I let out the smallest of sigh, a defeated sound.

"She caught me earlier. With Icarus."

Admitting even that—*just* that—flooded my cheeks with hot embarrassment.

Shiel's skin flooded too, but not from shame. No.

That softness leeched from him in an instant, replaced instead with a frigid coldness that froze me in place—even as he shrank back away from me, out of reach. He was still for a few moments, and when he finally spoke again, his voice had grown hard as stone.

"You were with him."

It wasn't a question, but it had the weight of one. It had the weight of a thousand questions. "Before you came to me, you were with *him*."

"I ... I was," I said. I wanted to look away, to turn away from the intensity of his gaze—but I couldn't. I couldn't do anything but answer truthfully. Now wasn't the time to start with lies.

I'd avoiding having to discuss the dark fae since we arrived, however narrowly, but the look in Shiel's eyes told me that time was over.

I felt my throat close up as I waited for him to demand more answers. To demand to know what happened while I was with Icarus.

"We didn't actually do anything. Just like I told you—Ada came, she interrupted us before it was too late—"

"So you came straight to me after? And had me take you to my bed, instead?"

I gaped at him, unable to say anything in response. I waited, in the silence, for him to say something else— anything else—but all he did was stare at me, his face a mask of disbelief and anger.

He stood, finally, his jaw set so firmly that I could see the muscles twitch beneath his skin.

"Was that what this was all about?" he growled now, voice barely more than a whisper. "Why you came to me?"

I shrank back from him, my eyes darting around the room as I tried to come up with the words to counter his accusation.

But nothing came.

Shiel's face darkened further, and he stepped away from me completely. He turned his head, looking away from me as if he could no longer stand to look at me and what I had done.

"I want to know what happened while you were with Icarus," he said finally, his voice low and full of anger. "Every detail."

My mouth opened, but I couldn't find the words. I couldn't find it in me to tell him how it felt to draw close to Icarus again, how it felt each time we were alone. How even though I knew everything about being with the fae Lord of the Wildness was wrong, I couldn't find it in myself to resist him.

Even when it meant risking the one thing I'd risked every-thing else for.

I couldn't answer Shiel, but that was answer enough.

"I knew it," Shiel hissed at me, a sharpness in his tone I'd never heard before. His golden eyes had taken on a light from within, a dangerous glow that made my stomach knot. I felt myself shrinking again. I wanted to curl up and disappear.

"You used me," he spat, his voice so low I almost didn't hear it. The accusation stung, and I felt tears prickling at the corners of my eyes.

"No," I whispered, my voice barely audible even to myself. "I would never do that. I didn't come here to—"

I tried to deny it, to explain—but it only made Shiel angrier. He stepped closer to me, his eyes blazing with fury.

"Don't lie to me," he spat out between gritted teeth. "I can see the truth in your eyes."

It felt like a slap in the face, because part of me had started to wonder if he was right. I wanted to apologize—to beg for his forgiveness—but all I could do was stand there, silent and ashamed. Had I come here to seek the comfort I couldn't get from Icarus? Was it the heat between me and the dark fae that had reignited, not one that had been growing between Shiel and I all these weeks?

Shiel's gaze softened slightly then, though the anger still simmered beneath the surface. He shook his head slowly, as if trying to find the words that would make sense of what had just happened between us. But no words came, nothing that could make this right again.

So, instead, he broke me further.

"You commanded me."

My eyes widened, his accusation so clear and so damning, it made bile burn at the back of my throat.

"How *dare* you?"

I croaked out the words like they were poison themselves. I was on my feet now, too, my skin burning hot with a rage that matched the fae lord before me.

"How dare you accuse me of that? Of forcing you."

"Did you not?" Shiel's answer came too fast. "How would I know?

My mouth hung open for a moment. "Because it's me, Shiel," I snapped back. "Because I wouldn't do that to you. You know me."

Shiel just tilted his head back so that he looked down at me, the outer corner of his mouth turning up slightly. "I thought I did."

The pain of his words stabbed into me as keenly as any blade.

He saw the pain on my face, the horror, and the rage on his face dimmed. He reached for me, tried to say something, but I wouldn't listen.

I left Shiel without saying anything. I turned on my heel and fled, ignoring his calls for me to stop. It was cruel, I knew, but not as cruel as his words that had lodged themselves into my steadily bleeding heart.

# CHAPTER THIRTEEN

I CHARGED OUT, SLAMMING THE DOORS OPEN WITH ENOUGH force to make the walls shudder. The roar of their closing echoed in my ears as I nearly ran straight into two guards marching past, barely noticing their stunned expressions until it was too late. One of the guards stepped up to block my way, a scowl firmly planted on his face.

"Is there a problem?" he demanded.

"No problem," I spat out the words. "Besides me, apparently."

Tears threatened to spill from my stinging eyes and take away whatever dignity I had left. He regarded me with pursed lips before glancing once at the door I'd just fled from and then back at me—dressed in nothing but the thinnest of silk shifts. I was too angry, too hot with rage to care about something so small as dignity, but that didn't stop heat from flooding my cheeks as he met his partner's gaze. They shared that brief confusion that all fae did when they tried too hard to place who I was until together, after a moment, the two of them finally stepped aside. That was all the invitation I needed to break into a run.

Desperate to avoid any other encounters on the way back to my rooms, I diverted through unfamiliar hallways, anything that would keep me clear of any more fae who might be wise enough to question why I fled.

Yet once again, fate seemed determined to test me. I knew this when I barged into another hallway and there she was— not Ada, but the source of the second voice that had so quickly set into motion the words that had sent me spiraling down this hallway to begin with.

I discovered the changeling princess surrounded by her courtesans dressed in lavish gowns and gaudy jewelry they had no right to be wearing this early. As if they were waiting for me all along, they slowly pivoted to meet my gaze, their eyes one by one trailing over the state of me. The sun had barely risen, and already the princess' court was in session.

It was the first time I'd encountered the changeling since I was forced to lift her from the glamour I'd first bound her to. At least the cuts and scrapes had healed, no sign remaining of the torture I put her through—not that she would remember it either way. This was hardly how I wanted to face her again, let alone the small court that she herself still somehow was allowed to keep. It was an insult, standing here before them.

I felt the heat of their scrutiny, but I didn't care. My anger was still too fresh, too raw, to let their judgment affect me. Instead, I focused on the changeling princess. She stood at the center of the group, her face twisted into a sneer as she looked me up and down.

"Well, well, well," she drawled. "Look who decided to grace us with her presence."

I barely registered her words, my mind still clouded by my argument with Shiel. But her tone was enough to snap me out of my daze.

"Though *grace* might not be quite the right word for it."

Her band of ladies sniggered behind upturned fans, each one giggling at this fresh insult. I stood still, refusing to speak as their mocking voices chorused around me like vultures that had just spotted a dead carcass. Fauna's tiara was particularly noticeable this time, towering over her head like it had been designed specifically to mock my insignificance. She stared at me with contempt expecting an answer. Instead, she received only a bored stare.

I had half a mind to leave without saying a word. I owed this creature nothing. She was a byproduct of my mother's cruelty, though I could hardly call her a victim of it. She'd lived a charmed life, the life destined for me, stolen from me. It was not her birthright that I now came to claim. If she knew I was here to take her life from her, then I might have at least felt pity for her.

But she, too, was now spelled under the glamour along with the rest of the castle. She knew not who I was, nor what I was here to take. This petty princess act was no act at all. She didn't sneer at me because she hated me for who I was, she simply sneered because that was who *she* was.

Fauna looked like she'd been looking for a chance to shuffle me into my place in her hierarchy here, but so far, I'd managed to avoid her. That seemed to only make her despise me more—for no other reason than the fact that I hadn't yet fallen into line beneath her. Now, however, was her chance, and from the wicked delight that glinted in her eye, she was eager to take it.

Her charmed life, stolen or not, had corrupted her.

At least it kept me from feeling guilt when I looked at her and knew her days masquerading as the true princess were numbered.

I should have left, should have taken the brand of a coward and turned back instead of confronting her, but that rage still burned too bright within me. So, instead, I met the changeling's gaze with steel and ice.

"What do you want, *Princess*?"

She tilted her head, the look in her eyes telling me I'd already made my first mistake. Beside her, her ladies-in-waiting giggled and whispered to each other, the sound grating on my already frayed nerves.

"I want to know what brings you to my presence, dear," Fauna said, her voice dripping with saccharine sweetness. "You seem ... disheveled."

The heat in my face had no right to deepen at her words, but it did.

I took a step forward, ready to lash out at her, but she held up a hand to stop me. "Oh, don't bother," she said with a suddenly exhausted sigh. "You're not worth the effort."

I gritted my teeth and tried to ignore the snickering that broke out behind her again. Fauna's eyes grew hooded as she looked me over again.

"Tell me, though, why are you here? Not *here*, here, in the corridors of my wing, but in the castle at all. I don't remember a proper introduction ... which can only mean one thing."

I let the silence hang between us until I had no choice but to take the bait.

"And what is that?"

At least the boredom had begun to take over my voice again, instead of anger.

"You're not significant enough to deserve one."

It was more bait, I knew it, but I took it anyway. The corners of my lips turned up in a smirk, one that I knew would irritate Fauna even more.

"Is that so?" I asked, feigning surprise. "And yet here you are, giving me a very personal introduction."

Fauna's sneer deepened as she took a step closer to me, her ladies-in-waiting moving with her like a flock of birds.

"I just wanted to make sure the new girl knew her place," she said, her voice low and menacing. "You're nothing but a commoner, a nobody, and yet you dare to walk around like you own this place."

I was starting to grow tired of this back-and-forth, but I knew I couldn't let Fauna get the best of me.

I leaned in closer to her, my voice low and dangerous. "I am more significant than you could ever imagine."

Fauna's expression shifted from haughty to curious. "Oh? And why is that? Is that why my mother has you sitting around with your face in books all day, studying ... what? The same stories I was taught as a child."

I could feel the eyes of her ladies-in-waiting on me, their giggles dying down as they sensed the change in the air.

I cocked my head to the side.

"Is that what this is? Are you ... jealous I'm getting the queen's attention?"

Fauna waved her hand dismissively. "Please, I'm the one wearing the crown."

I didn't know why that bothered me so much, but I felt my hackles raise. Of course, she was wearing the crown, I could see it now, glittering above my own face sneering before me. It was an ugly face when she wore it, and that made me even more angry, too.

"You may be wearing a crown now," I hissed at her, "but we'll see how long that lasts."

For a moment, there was stunned silence. Then, a ripple of laughter broke out amongst Fauna's courtiers.

"See how long that lasts?" Fauna repeated, her voice laced with amusement. "Oh my dear, is that a threat?"

I straightened my spine, holding her gaze with unwavering confidence. "Take it how you will."

I turned to go, finished with this useless encounter, when I was stopped by the low sound of something like a growl from deep down in the princess' throat.

"I didn't say that you could leave … turn around."

The command dripped from her mouth like acid so strong I had no choice but to do as she said, my feet slowly pivoting beneath me until our eyes met.

The way she looked at me, it certainly looked like she could spit that acid if she tried. Not that she needed to. The next words she spoke were biting enough on their own.

"Bow to me."

My brows drew together and my pride flared within me, "And why should I do that?"

Her brow raised. "Because I commanded you to, insolent girl. Now bow to me or I will have you cast out."

She lifted her chin, but so did I.

This was a test, I knew it. I could feel the entire room holding its breath, waiting to see what I would do. I could feel the power radiating from Fauna, and I knew if I bowed, it would be seen as a sign of weakness.

But I also knew that if I didn't bow, I'd have made another enemy within these walls.

There was a third option, of course. I reached inside myself for a moment, feeling for the wells of my glamour. I found it, my own glamour, more than enough to glamour the princess if I needed to.

But then I'd have to glamour all of them, and was that what I really intended to do? I had to pick my battles carefully, and relying on my glamour was a slippery slope. I'd already been accused of using my powers against one too many fae today.

Fauna had no right to demand such a thing from me—not when she had no idea who I truly was.

But then again, that was my own fault. I was the one who made her forget.

So, with that in mind, after a moment of silence, I did the only thing I could think of.

I did as she said.

I bowed.

It was a shallow bow, a mere nod of respect, but it was enough.

This newest insult only served to sprinkle further salt into the wound of Shiel's betrayal still freshly oozing in my chest. But at least, it had its intended effect. I could feel the tension in the room dissipate, and Fauna's face split into a cold, satisfied smile.

"That's better," she said, her voice dripping with arrogance. "Now, go. And remember, this is *my* palace."

She turned for a second to the courtiers at her back. "Things are worse than we thought if I'm having to remind my own subjects of that."

My heart pounded heavy in my chest at her words, long after she had gone. I had no good retort, nothing to throw back at her as the group erupted into dissatisfied whispers as they slowly moved away, leaving the hallway. I remained bowed, my head down, until the flush of shame finally faded. Eventually I straightened back up, only to be surprised to find that two of the courtesans were still there, staring at me.

The first was a female with hair the color of the night sky, her eyes the same dark gray of the rocky hills that sloped down to the outer city walls.

Then, she stepped forward, her voice barely a whisper. "You handled that remarkably well," she said quietly. "I've seen Fauna destroy a fae in fewer words. You know what they say about the crown and their gift with words."

I blinked, taken aback by her kindness.

"Thank you," I said. I hadn't expected to find kindness among the fae who lingered around the princess. Even less expected, however, was the sight of the second figure at her side … because it wasn't just any other female.

I hadn't recognized my sister in the crowd. She'd transformed, dressed in the trappings of the fae until she looked like another one of them. But she was still herself. Still human.

Most surprising of all, however, was that it wasn't hate or disgust on her face when she looked at me. It was pity.

Somehow, though, that was worse.

I hadn't seen her at first because of the gown she wore, so white she nearly melted into the white walls behind her. She wore a dress of the purest white, and for a moment we just stood there, staring at each other in silence until she finally broke it.

"You shouldn't let her treat you like that."

I didn't know what to say. I didn't deserve her kindness. More than that, I didn't understand it.

"You're better than this, Aurra," Ada whispered.

The sound of my name in my sister's mouth made something simultaneously skip and sink inside me. I had no reason to hope that she remembered me, but it was hard to look into the face I knew so well and know all she saw looking back at her was a stranger.

"Ada ... about earlier ..." I started.

She shook her head. "Stop."

Confusion muddled my mind even further. "But I owe you an apology."

Something strange crossed her face. She reached out as if to take my hand, but then stopped.

She glanced once over her shoulder, past the courtesan that had stayed with her, towards the place where the princess had now disappeared.

"You owe me nothing."

I was taken aback again. I searched her face, trying to understand what she meant, but I found nothing but a hollow feeling in my stomach. That feeling only grew and grew as I looked back at her. Maybe I didn't know this girl, this version of my sister, as well as I thought.

And that was the worst feeling of all, worse still than realizing she didn't know me.

It made me want to be selfish, to force her memories back upon her. Before I was given a chance to try, however, the courtesan at her side took hold of her sleeve and tugged her back towards the end of the hall where the others had gone.

I waited until the echo of their footsteps were gone too

before I let out a sigh and looked around me, the hallway, now empty except for me. If that was a test, I wasn't sure that I'd passed it, but I was sure there would be more to come.

I'd done more than enough of that already since I arrived here, in my own court.

No. Not my court.

Not yet.

But it would be soon, because Ada was right.

# CHAPTER FOURTEEN

My encounter with the changeling princess had at least reminded me of one key thing.

I was better than this, better than all of this.

I was the one with the power here.

The crown of the Eastern Court was mine to take when I wanted it. One word from me and it would be mine.

But one word—one wrong word—and we'd be plunged straight into a bloody prophecy, instead.

Fauna had reminded me of something I'd known from the very beginning, but I'd chosen to ignore. I'd chosen to believe that it was the confusion of the glamour I'd placed on the castle that made my tutor run me in endless circles. But they weren't instructing me. They were distracting me.

I needed to know the truth about what was happening outside these castle walls.

And I knew exactly where to start.

It was time to pay my mother, the queen, another visit.

If only it was that simple.

The castle was alive too early, a side effect of a court built around the rising of the sun. Even dressed appropriately, no longer just in the sheer silk shift I was so unfortunate to confront Fauna in, the guards at the door to the Queen's wing looked at me as if I might as well have walked in naked after sleeping with the pigs.

The guard cleared his throat, head facing steadily forward, eyes refusing to look at me when I asked for an audience.

"The queen isn't taking visitors today."

I glanced first at the door, then back at him, then down the hall—to where a trio of fae approached, clearly headed towards this door to do the very thing I was attempting to do, now. I wondered if they'd be given the same answer.

The other guard, stationed on the other side of the door, shifted slightly. His eyes followed mine, then flickered back to stare straight ahead.

I steeled myself, my voice sounding far surer than I felt as I declared to the guard, "I'm certain that my mother will be able to make time for me." I met his gaze head-on, challenging him not to dare hold me back. He looked at me a second time, and for a second, I saw his gaze grow cloudy as he took in the sight of me.

I was not the princess, he *knew* that, thanks to my own carefully placed glamour, but I looked like her. I knew I really looked like her, even if his muddled mind was trying to convince him otherwise. I held his gaze, challenging him to ignore that. I considered, even, using that same glamour to convince him further, but my challenge, it seemed, was enough.

With a shake of his head that didn't clear it, he finally relented enough to step into the throne room, shutting the door behind him with a soft click.

"What's going on here?"

The trio of fae had reached us. A tall male, dressed all in dark blue velvet, was accompanied by two females dressed the same. They had a distinct look to them that I couldn't place. They were fae, sure, but different from those I'd encountered from the other courts. Something about them didn't seem like they were from here, from my court, from the East.

The other guard, still standing at the other side of the door, glanced first at me, and then back at the leader quickly growing agitated before us.

"We have a meeting with the queen," he said. "Urgent business."

The guard still said nothing.

The man turned to me, and I felt my neck stiffen.

Thankfully, he looked at me a little too closely, and that same confused expression stayed his tongue. He and the two blue-clad females cast me a few sideways glances, but they said nothing. Together, we waited in tense silence. My heart thundered against my rib cage and sweat trickled down my temple. I'd been so determined to see my mother, to demand the truth from her, that I hadn't truly considered what exactly I would ask her. She wasn't the most forthcoming of fae. I doubted she'd give me any answers I didn't specifically ask her, no matter the threats I might make.

Did I even plan to make threats?

I hadn't come up with a strategy, exactly.

But, from the glance the first guard gave me as he appeared in the door once more, it seemed that lack of strategy had already come back to haunt me.

I knew, before he spoke it, I was not going to see the queen today. Not unless I was willing to force it.

He hardly gave me a glance as he took his post at the side of the door, forcing me to step back a bit as he did.

"The Queen won't see anyone else today."

He kept staring forward, even when the other three fae broke out in angry huffs.

"This is an urgent matter, most urgent. It can't wait."

They tried arguing with the two guards, but were given only silence in return.

I left them to their argument. Their voices carried after me until the echoes of them made their words jumble together into incoherent noise. I should have been angry that I'd been turned away, but instead, I simply felt that new resolve from earlier rise up in me again.

Sure, I could march back to those doors and use my glamour to command myself entry, command myself an audience. But I wanted answers, truthful answers that didn't require me to use the glamour the way Icarus had not just allowed me to but asked me to. I wasn't yet ready to rely solely on my powers. I knew it would be all too easy to grow lazy and complacent, to grow so dependent on them that they'd become a crutch.

But more than that, the reason I turned on my heel, was pride.

That pride could have easily gotten the better of me, but as I turned that next corner, already half determined to storm the rest of the way back to my rooms and sulk, I spotted something that gave me a much better idea. The fae that had interrupted my lessons with Phina yesterday had just stumbled out of a door himself, and upon spotting me, immediately got that same confused look that all the fae did when they tried to look at me too closely. He lost his footing and though he caught it, he didn't do it in time to stop the armload of scrolls he was carrying from tumbling out of his arms to scatter across the hallway.

He looked up at me, his face turning red with embarrassment. "I'm so sorry," he muttered as I approached, bowing his head in shame.

I stepped forward and bent down to help him gather the scrolls. "No need to apologize," I said, trying to mask the amusement in my voice. "Are these the scrolls that were missing yesterday?"

I had half a mind to thank him for the break his interruption had provided me. If it weren't for him, I'd probably already be roped into another sleep-inducing lesson. Though, then again, I also wouldn't have embarrassed myself beyond hope not once, but *three* times since then.

He looked up at me again, his eyes meeting mine as he seemed to struggle to remember me for a moment before I saw a flicker of recognition in his gaze.

I instantly regretted it.

"You shouldn't be here," he muttered, again. "Phina's been looking everywhere for you."

Of course she was.

One of the scrolls I reached for had started to come undone, and I saw some of the letters scrawled on there—it made me pause just long enough to read the top line before the fae beside me snatched it up and tucked it neatly into the pile of papers he'd regathered in his arms.

I recognized the handwriting at once, but I didn't have time to read it.

He saw me looking, and for a second, he hesitated before straightening up.

"These are for the queen's eyes only," he said, stiffly."

Of course they were, too.

"Those scrolls ..." I said, straightening up to. "Those are letters, aren't they? From Shiel's advisor, in the West?"

"Standard reports, nothing more," he said, but something about his voice sounded off. It was like he was repeating something he'd been told time and time again, but wasn't entirely sure he believed it himself.

"Is Shiel aware that he's sending reports to the queen?"

The advisor blanched a little. "Of course—"

I held out my hand. "Then you wouldn't mind if I took one of those to Shiel, would you? I've just seen him. He was asking about these directly. It would save you time."

Of course, he'd said no such thing and I had no such plan. The very last person I wanted to see right now was Shiel, but something about the scroll had seemed off. I couldn't quite place it, but it nagged at me in a way that refused to be forgotten.

For a second, he almost looked like he was going to relent. I took advantage of that.

"What's your name, again?" I asked, before he could deny me.

The question made him stumble over his words. It took him a second to answer.

"Newt."

"Newt," I repeated, cocking my head to the side as I batted my eyelashes, hoping I looked coquettish and not absolutely insane. "You've been working hard, looking for those scrolls. You look like you haven't slept a wink since I last saw you."

His mouth dropped open slightly and he struggled again to reply.

"I haven't actually," he admitted, shifting the papers in his arms. He let out a loud sigh and I could see the exhaustion etched on his face. "I've been running all over the castle trying to track them down. But they're important, and I can't let them fall into the wrong hands."

"Exactly," I agreed, holding out my hand. "I'll deliver them straight to Shiel."

He looked up at me, again then, the confusion clearing away slightly. "I'm not sure it's wise for you to be asking to see them."

"I thought you said they were standard reports."

His brow furrowed, the confusion replaced with suspicion.

"It's not my place to say," he said, his voice growing firmer. "But I think it would be best if you left these be and went back to your lessons."

I could feel my frustration mounting.

"I don't want to go back to my lessons," I said, crossing my arms over my chest. "I want answers."

Newt looked at me skeptically. "What kind of answers?"

"The kind that explain what's really going on here," I said, my voice growing louder. I leaned in toward him. "The kind you might be able to give me."

Newt's expression softened, and for a second, I saw a brief clarity in his eyes. "I understand," he said, his voice gentle. "But I don't think these letters are going to give you the answers you're looking for. Only the queen and her tutors know that, really."

"Tutors?"

As quick as that clarity was there, it was gone.

"Advisors," he said, but he hesitated before continuing, that cloud of confusion my returning stronger than before, if only for a moment. "I need to be going. I don't want to be responsible for putting thoughts in your head. You shouldn't be asking these kinds of questions."

He drew back from me, and I knew he was lost to me.

I patted his arm once more, watching as that blush deepened again. He looked pleased with himself as he strode away, his scrolls intact. Little did he know he'd given me all I needed to know, anyway.

Maybe fate was on my side after all, if only for today.

# CHAPTER FIFTEEN

I<small>F THE QUEEN WASN'T GOING TO PLAY FAIR, THEN NEITHER WAS</small> I.

"Phina, I didn't know you were one of the queen's advisors."

My tutor turned on her heel in surprise, the relief on her face short lived as she took in my own expression.

It was a half-cocked guess, a slip of Newt's tongue, but the moment I saw the shift in Phina's own face, I knew I'd guessed right.

That explained why she'd been chosen as my tutor. She was a horrible tutor. Hopefully she made a better advisor.

I knew the queen had weighed this game in her favor, but I had no idea just how much. It was time to start tipping the scales. I'd cast this glamour, and I'd finally strip it if I had to. This was my kingdom, crown on my head or not, and I had a right to know what was going on in it.

Phina tried to speak, but her expression didn't change as she struggled to save whatever secrets she'd been ordered to keep. She finally started to find the words, but I straightened, and as I moved, something in her shifted. She'd been afraid of herself before.

But now, as I rose and met her gaze, she was afraid of me.

It was as if, even before I lifted the glamour over her, she felt what I was about to do, sensed the change before it came.

"I release the glamour placed over you. Tell me, now, the truth."

Phina's eyes widened as the glamour lifted, and she stumbled back, almost falling over the chair behind her. She looked at me, fear etched onto her face, and I could see the panic in her eyes.

"I … I can't," she stuttered, taking a step back. "The queen, she ordered us not to say anything. I can't betray her trust."

I took a step towards her, my expression hardening.

"Her trust is not the one that should concern you. Besides, Phina … I think if you take a moment, you might realize the truth is no longer something you can keep from me."

My tutor opened her mouth to argue, but suddenly, she stopped. Her whole body froze, standing there unmoving except for the slowly forming shock that fell over her face as the last of the glamour's hold cleared from her mind.

Confusion replaced the shock next. She'd not been present when I arrived, not seen the magic I performed, and it was unlikely the queen or Eckhardt were so careless as to speak openly about me, even in front of the fae who were unable to understand my place thanks to the glamour I'd shrouded them with.

But doubtless, there were other things that had now begun to fall into place, memories from these last weeks that were only now beginning to make sense now that her mind was not under my spell's control—or, just as likely, more things that *didn't* make sense. Phina's eyes widened as the very last magic of the glamour dissipated. She took a step back and looked around, as if she had never seen the room before, her eyes drinking me in as if it was the first time she'd truly looked at me. She seemed disoriented, struggling too hard to regain composure that kept slipping further and further away.

"Princess!"

The word fell from her more like an accusation than anything else. Her face flickered between emotions so quickly that she looked like she was going mad. Eventually, however, despite the confusion and the madness, she had the sense to fall down to one knee, head bowed and voice dropped low.

"Your Majesty, I—"

"Don't call me that," I interrupted. "I'm not the princess you know, but it's too complicated to explain now. Just tell me what's going on here, in the Eastern Court? What's keeping my mother so busy, and why is Shiel's advisor sending reports directly to the queen, instead of him?"

Phina hesitated for a moment before finally speaking. She had no choice, of course, but in a way … I commended her efforts. Perhaps, one day, she could make such a loyal advisor to me, too.

"There are rumors, Your Highness," she said, at last. "Rumors of a rebellion brewing amongst the humans of Luxia."

"A rebellion?" I repeated. "But the humans, they're always restless. They've always hated the fae."

"Not here, in the Eastern Court," Phina said, cringing as

the answer came out all too easily. "The humans here live peacefully amongst us. Until lately."

Her eyes widened a little, as if something suddenly made sense to her.

"What is it, Phina?"

She clapped her hands over her mouth, her eyes widening even further. She struggled for a moment, muffled gasps choking her until she coughed out a glamour-bound reply.

"The king," she gasped. "Something's happened with the king."

Panic darkened her eyes as the memory, or perhaps a harsh reminder of something she'd once known but been forced to forget, settled in.

Ah yes, my dearly departed father.

Not for the first time, a small stab of something like grief pricked inside me. I felt no lost love for him. I never knew him, and from what little I'd begun to gather, he was something of a tyrant. It was hard not to be, with this power now passed on to me.

But he was my father, and now, I'd never know him.

I'd come home, but I'd come too late.

And from what Phina was telling me now, from the rumors that had been swirling about unrest and rebellion, I might be too late for the rest of my kingdom, too. Had the glamours he'd cast in his life broken with his death? Or had he simply been losing his grip in the days leading up to his death, the aftermath only felt long after his powers to keep the peace—however forcibly—were gone.

But even unrest amongst the humans couldn't be *that* concerning, could it? Rebellion sounded strong, but they were only humans.

152

We were fae.

"How bad is this rebellion, Phina?"

Once again, she struggled to keep from answering me, but once again, she failed.

"The queen has called the council. In a week's time, they'll meet to discuss how to proceed. I don't know the specifics."

"But you do know it's serious?"

The look on her face was enough of an answer.

A rebellion was brewing? Was it really so bad that the queen would call on the other courts now? Or was that just a guise, a ruse meant to call them here for my supposed debut? It would be one way to get them here without stirring too much suspicion.

But suspicion from whom?

From them … or from me?

That debut, the announcement that the king was dead and I would be taking his place, was starting to sound even less likely by the moment.

Before I had the chance to ask more questions, however, Finch suddenly appeared behind me, standing up from the ground with a groan as he stretched his neck first from one side, to the other. It was my turn to find myself completely disoriented.

"Sorry, Aurra, I've been trapped in that cat form for some time now. I needed a minute to stretch out a kink in my neck."

"How did you, how were you …"

My mouth hung open as he stepped forward, a devilish smile on his face.

"You hit me with the same glamour as the guards yesterday. Stay, remember? Don't move? Rather unfortunate for me.

Guess the spell was a little stronger on me as a cat, because I've been staying there, unmoving—just as you ordered, mind you—since the moment you left."

"But ..."

I trailed off, my eyes flickering to the space beneath my chair, where that cat had so often been. That cat, always winding around my ankles, sitting on my lap, curling up beside me when I went to bed.

Color rushed into my cheeks.

"You were here, all this time?"

His smile broadened. "I like to keep an eye on my girl."

His words made my blush deepen.

I was too shocked, or maybe too amused, to be angry. I'd wondered where Finch had gone off to, how he'd avoided being roped into the queen's bidding or Shiel's command all week. It felt comforting, knowing he'd been here, all this time, with me.

Finch leaned in a little closer. "If I'd realized you'd be this happy to see me, I'd have revealed myself sooner. And more of myself, too ... if you catch my meaning."

I swatted at him.

*That* finally broke the short-lived spell Finch's appearance had cast on me, but it was a moment too late. When I turned back to resume my interrogation, Phina was gone.

Somehow, she must have slipped from the room in the moments when Finch and I were distracted. From the silence on the other side of the hall, she'd taken the guards with her.

I swore as soon as I realized what had happened.

Perhaps Phina was a little *too* loyal to my mother for any hope she might switch sides.

There was only one place she was headed now. I'd wanted

an audience with the queen, but not under *these* circumstances. If she came for me now, it would be with demands. This time, before I decided whether or not I'd meet them again, I needed to know what I was really up against.

Was there truly rebellion brewing, or was my mother calling on the courts for more nefarious reasons?

"We need to get ahead of this."

"And how to we do that?" Finch asked.

I considered that.

"By finding out with our own eyes just what this rebellion looks like."

# CHAPTER SIXTEEN

I slipped out of the room, Finch trailing behind me, as we made our way through the winding halls of the faerie castle. We moved quickly but discreetly, trying not to draw any more attention to us than was absolutely unavoidable. It wasn't difficult. The castle was busier than usual, especially as we neared the main hall.

We'd no sooner slipped out into the courtyard, however, then we were accosted.

This time, for once, by a friendly face. Or, if not exactly friendly in the way it took in the sight of Finch so closely hugging my side, at least recognizable.

"Zev!"

The massive golden-haired fae stood like a wall before the both of us. His face was stern, but he was unable to hide that hint of something softer in his gaze that appeared whenever he looked at me. Like Shiel, his hair had grown longer too, half of it tucked up in a bun, but the rest cascading in waves until it reached well past his shoulders.

His shirt clung to him with the remnants of swear and

dust, his blade still hanging at his side from where he'd doubtless returned to sparring with the queen's guard.

Though I'd spotted him yesterday, the sight of him up close warmed me. It was the first time I'd seen him since we were parted in the queen's throne room, and I'd missed him more than I realized.

"What are the two of you up to?" he asked, eyeing the both of us suspiciously. For a second, his gaze flitted over our shoulders to search the darkness of the doorway at our backs. "I'm guessing Shiel doesn't know about this."

Shiel.

A knot formed in my stomach at the very mention of the Western Court lord.

We hadn't exactly left on the best of terms. In fact, there weren't many worse terms I could have left on when I strode from his bedchambers this morning. I'd let the lord take my innocence, and in return, he'd accused me of not only using him—but *coercing* him. He'd claimed I'd used my glamour, but that didn't make the accusations hurt any less than if he'd accused me of using physical force.

I'd tried hard not to think on it then, and I certainly didn't want to think on it now—not with Zev and Finch staring me down.

"Shiel doesn't need to know about this."

It was Finch who said it, but I was all too quick to agree. I reached out and caught Zev by the collar of his shirt, tugging him into the shadows along the edge of the white stone courtyard and out of the doorway, my voice dropping low so that anyone passing by wouldn't overhear.

"Either you can come with us, or you can keep quiet. Which will it be?"

Together, the three of us were able to make it out of the castle courtyard and into the innermost ring of the city without trouble. Zev had lent me his jacket and suggested I pull the hood up over my head, since only the castle had been glamoured to forget I wore the princess' face.

The innermost ring of the city was inhabited, at least it seemed, only by fae—those who worked but did not live within the castle itself. The houses were grand and stately, built from that same white stone of the castle. There were no markets here, but shops lined the corners selling fae food that made my mouth water. The palace kitchens had been quickly fattening me up in the little time I'd been there, but I didn't think I'd ever grow used to the faerie food.

The streets were manicured to perfection, the fae polite, and the presence of guards nearly undetectable. It felt safe.

The same could not exactly be said for the next ring of the city.

It was a stark contrast, the lives that were lived on the other side of the gate.

This was where the humans lived. Some fae lived among them too, but they were few and far between.

I knew this was the only faerie court where humans and fae lived side by side, but I had no idea how greatly they outnumbered us. The houses were smaller in this next ring, built from stone and brick that had been lime washed to match the fae homes and castle higher up, and though there were crimson panes of glass in some of their windows, precious gems were nowhere to be found.

Neither, however, were any signs pointing to rebellion.

Not, at least, until we reached the outer ring of the city.

Each ring of the city leading away from the castle was larger than the last.

I'd been inside the carriage, the city blacked out from my view, for most of the trip up from the city gates to the castle. Now, I wished more than ever that I'd not been.

I drew the hood close around my face as we trudged further out still from the castle itself. I would have gone to greater lengths to conceal myself had I known where our journeys would take us.

There were no other fae in this outer ring, none except the guards—of which, there were more than plenty.

The moment we stepped through the gates, it was as if I *felt* a shift in the air.

And I'd thought the contrast between the first two sections of the city was great.

The air was less sweet here, thicker with that ocean spray, but the salt that cut through the air in the higher rings seemed to hang heavy here.

What hung heavier still, however, were the spirits of fae and humans alike.

It should have been hard to find the signs of unrest and rebellion, but even the faces of the fae guards looked disgruntled as we passed. I looked to Zev and Finch to make sure I wasn't the only one who saw it, but from the way both of them drew nearer to me, I knew they saw it, too. We walked in silence for a while, the tension palpable as we made our way through the outer ring of the city. The streets were narrower here, the buildings smaller and far less manicured. They were lucky to have a potted plant outside, let alone the gardens and hedges that had brightened the higher levels of the city streets.

It was strange, in a way, to think that this was the only court where the fae claimed they actually got along with the humans that they ruled. This was also the only court where the humans remained at all. We'd burned down the rest of their cities and then built our own, leaving them with our scraps. No wonder they'd never risen up in all this time. There were too busy trying to rebuild, still.

I knew my power, the power of the Tongues was great, but was it really so great that it could keep an entire court in line for so long?

Was it really so great that without it, even for just a few weeks—three months at most—that the entire court, that the entire *kingdom* could be on the verge of crumbling?

All this I wondered before we even saw it, the first signs that Phina had not lied.

It was strangely, reassuring, the sight of this crowd. It was a sign my mother hadn't lied, that the letters she'd sent summoning the courts were, in fact, for this purpose—and not something more sinister.

Perhaps I'd been wrong to be so suspicious. The queen, for all her faults, hadn't yet lied about the bargain we'd struck. I was the one who was here, now, instead of upholding my own end.

That little reassurance, however, only lasted so long.

We didn't see the first signs until we left the main, winding street, and stepped out into the crisscrossing maze of alleys that made up most of the outer ring of the city. It was a massive city, far larger than the other courts I'd been to. Much larger than the human city where Shiel, Zev, Finch, and I had spent one fateful night so long ago. With a map, it would be difficult to traverse the full width of this outer ring within a couple hours. Without it, I could imagine getting lost for days.

Especially when the crowds began to thicken, pressed closer by the buildings set too near together.

The air grew heavier with every step we took. The buildings here were built with rough-hewn stone, the few once considered grand enough to deserve the white of a lime wash now so stained with dirt and salt and grime that they nearly matched the shade of their untouched neighbors.

The streets grew uneven and unkempt, debris piling in the corners and broken glass crunching underfoot. Most of the windows didn't even have glass anymore, just thin waxed paper to keep the wet sea air out.

But it wasn't the general disrepair that made the hair on the back of my neck stand up. It was the sense of tension that hung here, heavier even than the thick salt and brine, so thick it was almost tangible. We weren't the only ones that seemed to constantly be checking over their shoulders. Our voices weren't the only ones that dropped to hushed tones whenever a dark-clad figure passed too close.

All the figures were dark clad here.

If the sense of unease was a match, this entire ring of the city would already be on fire.

Faces turned towards us with growing suspicion the further into the ring we passed. I might have been able to hide my face, but there was no hiding the two fae beside me. They stood out among the humans that lingered here like glowing beacons.

Up ahead, at long last, we saw an actual crowd gathered. Even from a distance, the displeasure in their voices was thick enough to swim in. It was a gruel of restlessness and resentment.

The throng up ahead was gathering quickly, growing larger by the second. It was clear from the flurry of movement where the front of the crowd seemed to converge before a small, dilapidated market stage, that whatever tableau was about to play out was soon to begin.

Zev put his arm around me, tucking me further into the safety of his shadow.

"Are you sure you want to see this?" he asked. "This place, it doesn't look like it's going to stay so quiet for long."

I pulled the hood up tighter around my ears, and not for the first time, wished I had my old face back—the one that might not be so easily recognized. I'd grown far too comfortable in my new skin under the protection of the glamoured castle.

"That's an understatement," Finch said, still pressed closely to my other side. He too huddled close to the massive warrior with his arm now somehow slung over both of our shoulders. "This crowd looks like it's looking for a reason to turn into a riot, and whatever they're here to see hasn't even started."

I paused for a second to look up and down the streets branching beyond us to either side. While I looked, at first, for any sign of the guards I was sure would already be breaking up this gathering if they had the chance, my sight lingered on what it found in their absence.

Ever since we'd arrived in the human ring of the city, I'd been unable to keep a twinge of guilt from growing into something far greater inside me. I saw the poverty and desperation that plagued the people there, conditions that I'd grown familiar with in my own human life but had so quickly forgotten now that I was fae. Their homes were run down and dilapidated, with leaky roofs and broken windows. Children ran barefoot through the streets, their clothes ragged and torn.

It was a stark contrast to the luxury and opulence of the faerie courts. It was really no wonder that unrest was brewing.

And what I could see, I was sure, was only the beginning.

"I want to stay," I said, glancing up at Zev, and ignoring the tug of Finch on my sleeve. "I need to hear this for myself."

We moved as close as we could towards the outer edges of the crowd, but it soon became apparent we were anything but welcome here. The faces that turned our way quickly soured, their stares following us until we were out of view. It quickly became apparent that we'd have to find another way to view the spectacle, but luckily Finch seemed to be particularly skilled in this area.

Before I even had a chance to complain, he'd found a ladder squeezed tight between two houses that led up to a small construction platform overlooking the square on the other side. From where we sat, nestled tightly between two buildings on boards that sagged particularly beneath the two fae's weight, we had a clear view of the stage above the onlookers.

At first, I was worried that we'd be spotted, but no one was going to see us. Not when every face was trained forward towards the man that was now stepping up to stand in the middle of the stage.

The moment I laid eyes on him, I shrank back slightly into Zev and Finch. I knew, instinctively, that I should fear this man. I didn't have to see the stumps where his hands used to be to know who he was. Even from here, from this distance, I knew him.

And I knew whatever was about to come from his mouth was going to be dangerous.

It was a small wonder Rayner had lived to see this day. Though, one look at the state of him, and he could hardly be said to be *living*. He'd been a cruel twisted version of a man when I first met him, and now … now he was what a cruel, twisted man became when fate had been even crueler and more twisted to him. His face was a mask of rage, even when he rested. His eyes flitted across the crowd, brow drawn, tongue darting across cracked lips that foamed with fury. The moment he opened his mouth to let out an angry cry, the crowd responded.

From the way they jumped and pounded their fists on their chests at the front of the crowd, this was not the first time they'd heard Rayner speak. This was a performance, one that he'd mastered well.

He stood before them like a savior ready to lead them to the promised land, and from the way he drank in their praise, he knew it.

"Look at this, I think we've grown since last we met."

Cheers broke out among the crowd, their voices a deafening roar that echoed through the square. Rayner basked in it, his eyes scanning the faces before him, a smug grin spreading across his face.

"I see many new faces here today," he continued. "People who have come to join us in our fight against the oppressors."

The crowd erupted in cheers again, fists pumping in the air.

"We will not be silenced," Rayner yelled, his voice rising above the din. "We will not be oppressed any longer. The fae may think they rule this city, but they are wrong. We will take back what is rightfully ours."

The crowd roared its approval, and I felt a shiver run down my spine. Rayner was dangerous, and his words were inciting violence. As I looked around at the faces of the people in the crowd, I saw desperation and anger. They had been pushed to the brink, and they were ready to lash out.

I'd never been afraid of being a fae until that moment.

This was far worse than I imagined. There wasn't simply unrest in the city.

Rebellion had been the right word for it, and it was on the verge of breaking out. We might not even have a full week left.

"Many of you have heard what I have to say, or at least, you *think* you have, but I come to you today with news. I come to you with word from another kingdom, from the land that lies beyond our Western courts."

Another man stepped up onto the platform brandishing a scroll high above his head.

The crowd fell quiet at that. Bodies pressed closer as it was unfurled and held out for those closest to the front of the crowd to read what was written upon it.

"We've talked long of fighting back against the fae of Luxia," Rayner called out, "but talk is cheap. Our neighbors have decided they've had enough. Our neighbors now ready for war."

Whispers broke out amongst the crowd until one brave soul called out.

"But there are no fae in the western lands."

"No," Rayner agreed. "Not until recently."

A heavy silence fell, stretching deeper as Rayner moved to stand at the very edge of the platform.

"The boundaries between faerie and the human realm have been breached, again," he said, the crowd so quiet now he barely had to raise his voice. "If we do not act soon, it won't just be our own courts we need to contend with. If we don't act soon, more fae will come from their realm and they will push us out just as they did so long ago. But we have nowhere else to go."

I felt both the fae behind me stiffen. I glanced back at them, and for the first time, I saw true fear on both their faces. When their eyes scanned the crowd now, something had shifted within them. Not just Zev and Finch, but the crowd, too.

I saw their anger darken, turn murderous.

Panic began to rumble through the crowd.

I felt it, too.

More fae? From other realms?

When I looked back up at Rayner, my stomach twisted, and I had to fight the urge to be sick. I never thought I'd have to look at the stable master's ugly face again, but here I was. Rayner had only just begun to speak, but I'd already heard enough.

More than enough.

I turned to Zev and Finch again, my heart pounding in my chest. Apparently, I wasn't the only one who thought so.

"Uh, Zev …"

Finch's whisper drew both of our eyes towards the cramped street behind us. The crowd continued to thicken, spreading out into the narrow side streets too. Soon, the crowd would grow too thick for us to even consider an escape. And from the sound of the crowd already, the last place I wanted to find myself was trapped in the middle of a thousand humans chanting for my kind's demise.

They were not under my glamour, after all. They'd take one look at me and know who I was. I'd make a pretty prize to start out their rebellion.

I wasn't sure my glamour had recovered enough to stop a thousand angry humans from tearing me, or the fae at my side, limb-from-limb in their current rage.

"Right. Let's go." Zev took hold of me tight, and before I even knew what he was doing, he'd thrown me over his shoulder and hopped down between the buildings to the narrow alley, skipping the extra step it would take to use the ladder altogether. By the time we were straightening up and I was pulling my hood back over my head, Finch was just scrambling down behind us.

Zev's grip tightened on my arm, his head suddenly straightening as he spotted something in the distance a moment before the rest of the crowd did, too.

"We need to get out of here," he said urgently.

But we were too late, already.

Guards poured in from the outer corners of the city, their swords drawn, and the crowd scattered like rats—us among them. We had no choice. The moment the silver armor glinted in the light, the entire crowd surged.

Zev barreled at the head, holding me tight as Finch kept close at my heels. We were a formidable force amongst the crowd, but too noticeable. We avoided the guards, dashing out into the outer streets, but as soon as the crowd thinned enough for the panic to die down, a new kind of fear took hold—the kind that was filled with hate.

In the turmoil, my hood had fallen back. I noticed almost right away and went to pull it up, but I was too late.

I'd been recognized.

"Princess!"

The man's shout turned heads, first at him, and then directly at me. Zev and Finch froze beside me unsure of what to do.

His should drew the attention of a guard, who took one look at me, and then his brow furrowed. "It's a trap," he said. "The princess wouldn't be out here."

The guard shoved his way towards us, face stern, hand on the hilt of his sword. "You there, what are you doing? What kind of trick is this?"

He never reached us, however.

The crowd, incited by Rayner's rage, surged towards us. They overtook the guard first, pulling him to the ground and tearing his weapons from him.

In that instant, the crowd shifted. They swelled towards us, angry voices rising as their feet stampeded in our directions.

More guards started to converge then, too, but that drew even more rioters.

Because that's what the crowd had become.

In the momentary distraction, Zev grabbed me, threw me over his shoulder once again, and ran. By the time we'd worked our way out of the district, we were half lost some-where in the outer ring, but we were anything but safe. Word had spread fast that the princess was out amongst the rioters.

Guards and rioters alike stalked the streets, weapons in hand, looking for me.

I didn't know which one I feared more.

I felt something icy run through my veins every time I thought of the guard. Why had his first thought been to assume I was an imposter? I thought we'd made sure that rumor died?

I supposed even the glamour I'd placed wasn't perfect, but that presented us with a new problem.

The sun had long since set by the time we reached the doors to the second ring of the city, only to realized they'd shut with the sun. It would be nearly impossible to make it back to the castle without drawing attention to ourselves now.

The three of us crouched for a long moment between an overturned cart in another cramped alley. All the alleys in the outer ring had started to look the same. The sounds of the riots had started to die down, though I wasn't sure if that was because they'd actually been quelled, or if we'd just finally worked our way far enough away from them.

Either way, it wasn't until that moment that I found myself panting for breath between Zev and Finch, that I realized how exhausted I'd become—or how long we'd been running and hiding, ducking through these streets of my city, just to keep my own people from tearing me apart. As if sensing the way my heartbeat quickened, still, Zev put his arm over my shoulder, pulling me into him. Finch somehow wormed his way beneath his arm as well, on my other side, and pressed his face into the hair at the back of my head. He took a deep, steadying breath before he finally voiced what the rest of us were thinking.

"Unless we want to sleep on the streets, we'd better find an inn."

"Yeah," Zev said, glancing up and down the alley. "If we can find one in this ring tonight that isn't ready to lynch the next fae that steps foot inside."

# CHAPTER SEVENTEEN

THE DISTANT SOUNDS OF THE CLASH WERE BARELY A MEMORY BY the time we found an inn where Finch was able to secure a room for us. Even then, he was only able to do it by bribing a beggar boy to purchase it for us, and then—just to be safe—I used a little glamour to make him forget he'd helped us at all.

For once, I felt no guilt at all using my glamour.

I collapsed into the inn's bed expecting for exhaustion to instantly claim me, but instead, I felt the opposite. A surge of energy raced through me, causing me to sit back up so quickly that it startled Zev and Finch, both still unlacing their boots at the bottom of the bed. Their heads snapped towards me, their hands reaching for their weapons in alarm.

I held out my hands to reassure them, but there was nothing reassuring about the breathlessness that had taken over my voice.

"What ... what was that we just heard?" I asked, my brain only just now processing what it was Rayner had been saying, now that the immediate threat to our survival had passed. "What did he mean when he said that the veil between the realms had been breached?"

Both Zev and Finch looked at each other, and I knew from the pause that followed, that I was not going to like their answer.

"Rayner ..." Finch started, glancing nervously at Zev for support, and then back to me. "He was talking about Avarath. About Faerie."

*Avarath has turned its eye.*

A shiver ran down my spine at the sound of the familiar name.

There it was, the prophecy again. The harder I tried to avoid it, the more unavoidable it seemed to become.

Once again, as I closed my eyes, I saw that images of the bodies piling higher and higher. I tasted iron at the back of my tongue and smelled the warm scent of blood. I never wanted to see that image again, but once again, it haunted me.

I sat at the edge of the bed, my arms wrapped around my knees, as the two fae finished kicking off their boots. I hadn't bothered undressing yet, but I found myself unable to move from where I sat, hunched over, as if barely holding myself together.

The unrest that we saw tonight, that was not something that had happened overnight. That was the kind of unrest that had been brewing for some time. The queen could have mentioned this to me when we made our first bargain, she could have told me that the other courts had been called. It would have been a useful bargaining chip on her part. She'd warned me that the other courts might rebel, but she'd said nothing of the people that were already in the throes of it.

What could be her purpose?

Did she not want to admit her own weakness, her inability to keep her people in line in the weeks since the king had died? But couldn't she have instructed me to put the people under a glamour too, to calm them, as my father surely had? That was the only explanation I could think of for why this rebellion was happening now. There had always been unrest in the humans of this realm, I'd seen it all too often with my own eyes growing up among them. But it had never come close to this.

The king's influence must have been terrible.

I thought back to the dilapidated houses, the conditions that the humans of this city were expected to live in, while all the while sitting in the shadow of the opulent lifestyles of the fae that had taken this city from them to begin with. There was no way they'd lived here, all this time, like this, willingly.

"Aurra?"

Finch's voice, softer than usual, tore me from my thoughts. He knelt before me, one hand outstretched. It took me a moment to understand what he meant, but his gentle hands nudged me in the right direction. He took my foot and moved it to press in the middle of his chest while he began to undo the laces one by one.

"What are we going to do, next?"

"We have to do something about the people. We can't let them destroy the city, can't have men like Rayner stirring this kind of dissent, but what if he's right? What if there's even more to worry about then there obviously already is?"

Zev glanced at me in confusion. "What do you mean?"

"Well, clearly, they have a point about being oppressed," I said.

Finch's brows furrowed next and he paused halfway down my boot laces. "They're humans, Aurra."

I shot him a look that shut both of them up.

"And I lived as one of them for all of my life, up until a couple months ago," I snapped back. "I don't think there's anything wrong with having empathy for them. They're not so different from us, you know."

With all our glamour, there had to be a way to change the dynamic of our kingdom. There had to be a way for the humans and the fae to live in harmony—aside from me using my dubious glamour to force them into line.

"Look at you, already thinking like a queen," Zev said, as if reading my thoughts. His hand reached out to cup the side of my face for a second. The touch softened something inside me, and as I looked up to meet his gaze, the rest of me started to melt too. "You're going to make a better ruler than all the rest. I have no doubt about that."

Finch caught my eye next held my gaze as he removed first my left boot, then my right.

"The queen's already called her council," he said. "Now that you know what's going on, maybe you can work on it together."

They were right. Maybe this could be a chance for me to really prove myself, something beyond studying endless, drole lessons. My spirits had already begun to lift by the time I felt a second pair of hands reach for the complex laces of my dress behind me.

At long last, that burst of energy that had sent my heart racing had finally begun to fade. It was only then that I looked around the room and found a familiar sight.

Three fae. One bed.

I almost laughed aloud, and might have, if it wasn't so funny as it was surprisingly comforting.

"Just so you know," Zev said, his lips pressing close to my ear as he undid the last of the laces, freeing me from the corset I hadn't even noticed had been digging into my ribs, "Finch asked specifically for a room with one bed."

"Of course, he did."

"What can I say?" Finch asked, with a shrug. "I'm a hopeless romantic."

"Desperate for human touch, more like," Zev muttered.

Finch didn't deny that, either. "The closest I've gotten in ages is a few pats on the head, and that was when Aurra thought I was a cat."

A soft laugh bubbled up out of me, banishing away the rest of that cold fear that had almost taken over of me. I'd forgotten all about that.

In the midst all the recent stresses, I'd forgotten what it was like to laugh like this, to feel at ease in the company of these two fae the way I only did with them. It was like nothing had ever changed since that first night in the inn, like we were still those carefree fae that had known nothing of the terrible mess we were about to walk into.

But there was no going back to that now. We were still in the very beginning of it now, but we were too deep in to turn back. Whatever was coming was already set into motion, whether we liked it or not, we were a part of it.

And yet, despite all that, there was something about being in this room with them that made me feel like maybe, just maybe, we could still hold on to that moment from not so long ago, if only for now.

If only for a night.

It was clear that things were about to shift yet again in this already unsteady world I was about to inherit. We might not have to deal with the consequences of a rebellion tonight, but we would soon.

And there was no telling what changes that might bring.

I was the one to break the silence that had settled over us, my voice low as I spoke. "I don't want to sleep, not just yet."

Zev's hand moved to my waist, fingers pressing into my skin in a way that sent shivers down my spine. "What do you want, Princess?"

It only sounded right on his lips.

It sounded so right I melted back into him, leaning my back into his chest as a heavy sigh escaped my lips. I laid there for a long moment before turning to face him, my fingers tracing the outline of his jaw. In answer, I placed my hands on his chest, my fingers brushing along the open neckline of his shirt where it met the heat of his skin. Without hesitating, I moved my hands downward until I found the bottom of his shirt and then pulled it up, over his head, only to freeze.

I'd been wrong before.

Most of his tattoos had faded, yes, but one remained.

One alone.

My name somehow remained scrawled along his ribs.

My eyes lifted to meet his, my lips parting. "But ... how?"

"Where do you think I went whenever I wasn't with you?" Finch chuckled. "I never would have left your side if I hadn't promised this one here I'd keep it going."

I felt my heartbeat quicken, and with it, my throat tightened as Zev lifted his hand to feel the beat of it beneath his fingertips. The bond between Zev and I hadn't been broken after all.

The air grew charged with a different kind of tension. Everything changed so quickly, I didn't feel the moment it tipped over the edge, only that after so many times it had come close before, it finally did. I wasn't sure who made the first move, only that suddenly there were lips pressed against my neck and hands sliding down my body.

It was all the permission I needed, and without another word, I began to undress the two of them, my fingers fumbling blindly with buttons and laces as their lips crashed into mine, onto my cheeks, my neck, my shoulders, my breasts. We moved together, all three of us, a tangle of feverish kisses, until we were all gasping for breath. At some point in the heat of passion we'd done away with the last of our clothes, now finding ourselves with nothing between us but our own sweat and skin. Deep desire, primal and all-encompassing, had flushed any other thought from my head except for the need to be with the two fae here with me, tonight.

It was Zev who eventually pushed me back onto the bed, his body hovering over mine as his fingers traced patterns over my skin. His arousal came to rest on my stomach, hard and enormous, just like the rest of him. Just the sight of it made me gasp and slick need begin to pool between my thighs. I'd felt the shape of him before, on a night not so unlike this not so long ago, but it was bigger than I imagined. Bigger than it should be.

"How is that going to fit?" I couldn't help but gasp out the question.

"Don't worry, Beautiful," Finch whispered. "We'll make sure it does.

His promise made my body ache even more.

"You are beautiful, you know that," Zev murmured, his lips finding mine in a heated kiss. "So beautiful, I lose my breath sometimes."

Finch slid to the top of the bed and pulled my head up so the back of my head rested in his lap. He brushed the hair away from my face as he looked down at me, his face aglow as he took in the sight of me.

"Gods, we're so lucky."

Zev positioned himself between my thighs as Finch's hands moved to massage my shoulders, then my chest, loosening the tension at the top of my breasts.

"Don't worry, he'll be gentle," he whispered to me. But then he leaned in closer, to add, "At least, at first."

The tip of Zev's cock pressed between my thighs, to the outside of my sex, but didn't go in. Not right away.

Finch bent forward, sliding his hands along my stomach until they met my thighs. He nudged them further apart, pulling two pillows to slide beneath them, and then ordered me to relax.

I took a deep breath and did as he said, urging the muscles between my legs to release just as Finch's fingers moved to start slow circles along the apex of my thighs.

Pleasure bloomed at his touch, Finch's pointer finger forming soft swirls around my clit as Zev pressed himself against me a little harder. With a moan, I felt myself starting to stretch, to let Zev into me little by little, every centimeter of him making the core of me twitch and tighten with pleasure.

Zev stopped, sweat already dripping from the tip of his chin. His breath had shortened.

"Relax," Finch reminded me. His second hand moved to cup my head, to readjust it where it lay on his lap. I could feel his cock hardening beneath me, hear his breath grow shorter too with his own excitement. "Come now, Aurra, be a good girl for Zev and let him fill your cunt."

The words brought a blush to my cheeks, but I complied, my hips arching up to meet Zev as he pushed himself deeper into me. My body shuddered and my eyes shot open, overwhelming sensation rocketing through me as I felt every inch of him.

Finch's hands moved down my body, one grasping my breast, the other pulling the pillow further beneath my hips, to give Zev better access to me.

"Yes," Finch whispered, his voice a low growl. "Take her, Zev. Show her what we can do together."

Zev moved slowly, allowing me to adjust to his size. His hands gripped my hips, pushing me up into his thrusts, each one growing harder and deeper.

Finch's hands ran over my body, teasing the soft, sensitive skin of my breasts and belly. His touch was gentle yet electrifying, sending sparks of pleasure through me with every stroke.

And that pleasure was quickly building, so intense it was almost too much to bear. I felt both of them, Zev deep inside me and Finch's fingers caressing my skin, and it soon felt like I was going to explode. Finch's hands kept moving on my body, helping push me closer and closer to the edge. Finch began to touch himself, his hand stroking up and down the length of his own cock as he watched and teased Zev and I until he was whimpering with his own release.

My cries grew louder and more desperate as I let myself go, my nails digging into Zev's back as I felt the wave of pleasure break over me. I heard Finch moan my name as his other hand moved to cover my mouth, muffling my screams as I rode out wave after wave that consumed me.

The intensity of my orgasm sent shockwaves through my body, my back arching off the bed as I trembled. Zev followed shortly after, groaning loudly, his whole body shaking as he came.

I found myself being pulled into a tight embrace between the both of them, the three of us intertwined together.

I found my lips near Finch's ear, and I pressed a soft kiss into the skin behind it.

"Does this mean you're now free?" I asked him. "Free of your faerie deal?"

He turned then and took my face in his hands. "I never made that deal intending to be free of it."

# CHAPTER EIGHTEEN

WE SLEPT ENTANGLED TOGETHER ALL NIGHT, EXHAUSTION holding all three of us so tightly in its clutches that none of us woke until it was already almost too late.

We heard the sound of voices outside, but it wasn't until the thunder of footsteps preceded a loud knock on the door that we were pulled out of our slumber. Even then, if it weren't for the voice on the other side of the door, we probably would have ignored it. But there was one voice not one of us would ignore, and it was the one that shouted out to us so urgently now.

"Let me in, all of you, or I'll break the door down."

It was Shiel.

Finch leapt from the bed and grabbed his clothes, hastily throwing them on and pushing me behind him protectively. I scrambled to get my own clothes on, my heart racing in my chest as Zev stumbled to the door to unlock it, not bothering with his own clothes, yet.

Shiel stormed inside just as I was pulling my shift over my

head, and I was grateful for it, because though his eyes immediately went to me, mine went to the fae male that had
accompanied him ... because Shiel had not come alone.

It took the Lord of the Western Court all of three seconds
to take in the scene and understand the sum of it. A blank
look fell over his face, but he said nothing, only straightened
up further.

"We have to go, now."

"How did you find us?" Finch asked, still struggling to
tug his foot into one of his boots–the wrong one.

Shiel just cocked his head and glanced with annoyance
between the two fae, before his gaze finally settled back
on me.

"The boy you glamoured was not the only one who saw
you last night," he said. "You're lucky he went to the guard,
and not the rioters, or you might not have been woken so
graciously this morning ... if you were lucky to wake at
all."

Embarrassment colored my cheeks as Shiel shamed us for
our carelessness.

He was right, of course, but that didn't stop his patron-
izing tone from making my temper flare.

I was fully aware of how I looked, of what state I was in
when I turned to face Shiel, my dress still slung over one arm
and my hair a wild mess of sleep around my head. I didn't let
it stop me from meeting his rigid gaze and even more rigid
posture.

"We did nothing wrong," I said.

"Zev and Finch are my men," he retorted. "They're
supposed to remain by my side."

"So, you would rather I have gone out on my own?"

Shiel stumbled over his own words for a moment before he finally settled on, "You shouldn't have gone out at all."

Behind Shiel, the fae that had accompanied him cleared his throat.

"Excuse me Lord, Princess ..." he started, bowing to the both of us as he turned our attention to him, however reluctantly. "But there will be time for this later. Time is of the essence, here."

Something about his tone, about the way that Shiel's face darkened again, turning stony serious, made my own rage fade.

"This is my advisor," Shiel said, nodding once in thanks to the other fae. "And he's right. We have to leave. All of us. Now."

Zev, Finch, and I exchanged glances before nodding in agreement. We gathered our belongings and finished dressing as fast as we could, while Shiel waited by the window, his face practically pressed to the glass as he kept watch. His advisor waited below, his footsteps practically wearing a groove in the stones down below.

As we made our way out of the inn, I felt my insides quiver with apprehension. I had no idea what was going to happen next, but I knew it wouldn't be good. We made our way through the city in silence, and even though I felt like I should have been relieved, I couldn't help but feel a deep sense of dread. It was the first time I'd seen Shiel since I last stormed away from his accusations. I wondered, as we followed after him and his advisor, if he still thought I'd glamoured him.

My stomach still twisted at the very idea that he thought me capable of that.

A change had settled over the city since the night before. It wasn't until we reached the gate to the next ring of the city and found it closed, a long line stretching towards a small door at the side, that anything actually seemed amiss, however. The line stretched so far down the street that I didn't see the end of it. Humans and fae made up those waiting, but even in just the short time it took us to approach, I saw no human given entry. The guards at the door looked exhausted, their faces taking a few seconds to recognize us when we approached, Shiel and his advisor leading the way straight to the head of the line instead of settling in at the back.

A few grumbles broke out from the crowd until I turned my head, hidden again under my cloak, and a few faces recognized me still.

I just hugged the cloak tighter and followed along as Shiel ushered me inside to the next ring.

It was quiet here, too.

The few fae that had made it through the gate had long since disappeared, or were already well up the winding road leading up towards the innermost tiers of the city.

I let my eyes wander for a moment, taking in the almost eerie stillness that had settled over the city, and then I felt a hand on my arm that pulled me towards the west.

Shiel's gaze was hard as he looked at me, and he spoke with an urgency that I'd never heard before.

"Come," he said. "We're already late."

He was already several steps ahead of me before I stumbled after him.

"What's going on, Shiel," I asked. "Late for what?"

Behind me, I heard the others hurrying to catch up as they were ushered in through the gates after us, one by one.

Shiel didn't respond right away, however, just kept trudging onward. I glanced back at Zev and then at Finch. The advisor was still at the gate, his papers getting checked.

I hurried my footsteps to catch up to Shiel, but it was difficult to match his gait without having to practically run to keep up.

"What is it?" I repeated, a little breathless. The city streets here sloped upwards, and I'd grown used to sitting at a desk studying for a little too long.

"The city has gone into lockdown after last night's riots."

The answer was simple, too simple. I knew from how he refused to look at me that it was not the real answer, and he knew it too.

"No, Shiel," I said, catching his arm just long enough to make him slow for a second. "That's not what I meant."

He ignored me, just shook me off and kept walking.

I stood, stunned for just a moment, before I took off after him again. The others had almost caught up to us now.

He kept his head straight, refusing to so much as acknowledge my existence even when I caught up to him again.

"Come on," I snapped, finally, when he refused to budge. "Tell me, Shiel, what's going on. As your future queen, don't make me order you."

He stopped then, finally, and suddenly. His head snapped to stare me down as he growled out his answer.

"Why not glamour me, instead?"

My jaw fell open.

I took a step back from Shiel, the shock of his accusation

hitting me like a physical blow. The hurt and anger that had been simmering inside me since our last encounter bubbled to the surface, and once again, it was too much to force it back down.

I was the one to storm off this time.

I was almost surprised when he followed, more surprised still when his hands caught hold of my shoulders and forced me to a stop.

"I'm so sorry, Aurra," he said, breathless, my feet barely done moving by the time his hand was on me this time. He kept one hand on me as he slipped to stand before me, his other hand tilting up my chin a bit to force me to look up at him in his eyes. "I know you didn't glamour me. You would never."

He stopped and looked up briefly. I heard the others' footsteps fast approaching.

"I came to you to apologize, but then ..."

His face reddened, the mask that was his usually composed face slipping as he admitted, "I saw you with Zev and Finch, and I don't know what came over me."

I could see the sincerity in his eyes, and I felt myself soften, almost melt into his touch as his hand stayed on my chin.

"I'm sorry too," I said softly. "I never meant to hurt you, Shiel. I never meant to make you feel used."

I stared at him, my heart racing at the feel of his hand on my chin. The intensity of his gaze was almost too much to bear, and I found myself leaning into his touch despite myself. It was the first time since our argument that I had let him get close to me, and I felt my resolve crumbling with each passing moment.

He leaned in closer, his lips just inches away from mine. I

could feel his breath on my face, warm and inviting. I closed my eyes and leaned in, wanting nothing more than to feel his lips on mine.

But then, just as our lips were about to touch, we heard a loud noise coming from the direction of the faerie court. Shiel's eyes widened, and he pulled away from me, his hand dropping from my chin.

"We have to go," he said urgently, grabbing my hand and pulling me along with him.

But then he let go of me and stepped back, his gaze flickering to the ground for a moment before he spoke again.

"The truth is, I don't know what's going on," he said, his voice low and strained. "All I know is that the queen has called an emergency council."

I hesitated then. "I thought they were coming next week."

The look he shot me was one of confusion. "Next week?"

"Didn't you know?"

Shiel's brow furrowed in answer, and my gaze shifted to land on the advisor now trudging up on Zev and Finch's heels.

Maybe the letters he'd been sending had been meant for Shiel, not the queen. That would explain why Shiel hadn't heard of the council meeting.

Unless, of course, there was a far more nefarious reason for Shiel not to have been called, too.

There was no time to dwell, however.

For once, the queen and I could agree on one thing. This matter of the riot had to be deal with, urgently. There was no time to waste. The last thing I wanted was for civil war to break out before I even had the chance to take credit for it.

"I think … I think I might have an idea of what's going on," I said. "It's more than just riots, Shiel."

I told Shiel everything we'd heard and seen the night before as we set off again. The others fell into step behind us, their faces grave with worry. The city streets were almost deserted now, the only sounds the soft whispers of the wind and the distant rumble of thunder.

We made our way up the winding path towards the court, our footsteps echoing loudly in the stillness. My heart was pounding in my chest, and I could feel the weight of Shiel's gaze on me as we walked.

Finally, we reached the gates of the court, and I felt a shiver run down my spine as I caught sight of the guards. They were heavily armed, their faces set in hard lines as they scanned the road, their eyes settling on us. I didn't remember there being so many when we left the day before. It was just a precaution, with the riots, but knowing that didn't stop my stomach from turning at the way their eyes lingered on me, in particular.

Shiel stepped forward, his hand raised in a gesture of greeting. Their faces were stony, but they stepped aside and allowed us to enter the castle courtyard.

"This way," the advisor muttered, urging us down an unfamiliar hall. As we followed after him, I could sense the tension in the air. Everyone was on edge, and I could feel the weight of the glances thrown our way as we passed. It was as if they were waiting for something to happen, something that would change everything. It wasn't just the city that had changed last night. Something had changed here too, but it wasn't until we reached the council chamber and threw open the doors that we realized what it was.

It was a moment later, a moment after the doors swung shut behind us and unfamiliar guards stepped in, that it all fell into place.

We'd just walked into a trap.

Shiel knew, the same moment I did, that we'd been betrayed. It wasn't until a moment later, however, that we realized just how badly.

And by then it was already too late.

# CHAPTER NINETEEN

I'D NEVER SEEN THE COUNCIL CHAMBER BEFORE, AND IF THE FAE who's faces turned to look at me as I stepped inside had any say in it, I never would again.

The council room existed just above the throne room, so that both of their windows faced towards the east. I imagined, in times when the court gathered down below, that you could hear the rumbling of their whispers, the tremor of their many footsteps.

All there was now, however, was silence.

At the far end of the room was a small balcony that overlooked another courtyard, this one stretching from one side of the castle to the other along the edge of the sea. The eastern sun still hung low enough to cast a silver morning glow around the silhouette of the one fae standing before us.

The chamber was dominated by a square table in the center, formed by the same white limestone as the white walls of this mausoleum of a castle. A compass rose had been carved into the middle each point designating a seat at the table for each court.

Two of the seats were empty, but it was the second occupied seat that first made uncertainty stab deep inside me.

Seated in the Southern Court's chair was not Lady Phyrra, the queen's sister and rightful lady of the court, but a stranger. Then, before Shiel could seat himself in his own seat, his advisor stepped up and took it instead.

That was when every nerve in my body froze.

"What is this?" Shiel demanded, his hand automatically reaching for the sword strapped to his side. He didn't have time to draw his blade before a second figure, Princess Fauna, stepped out from the queen's shadow and fixed him with a glare.

"Lay down your weapons."

It took me a second to realize what she was playing at.

What was this? Some farce? Was she really pretending she had *my* glamour?

A laugh had half clawed its way up my throat before it died, instead.

To my horror, I watched as not only Shiel, but Zev and Finch stopped in their tracks, their hands frozen on the hilt of their weapons for a long moment. They remained there, unmoving, as if they fought with an invisible enemy.

I could sense the fear emanating from them, and I knew that something had gone terribly wrong. I stood there, staring at them in shock. I couldn't believe that they had been so easily subdued. Was Princess Fauna actually controlling them somehow? That was impossible.

She turned her gaze towards me, and I felt a chill run down my spine.

*Unless ... of course.*

Princess Fauna might not be the heir to the throne like she pretended to be, but she was an Eastern Court Fae.

A fae that, up until a couple months ago, had no glamour. A fae that could now channel the same dark glamour that had left both Icarus and I blackened and burned, without the same trouble.

My head snapped back to stare at the princess, but that was my mistake. I should have been watching the queen. By the time I'd fully understood the stakes of the tableau playing out, one of the guards lunged forward and struck me hard in the center of my back, knocking the wind from me.

At the same second, the doors flew open and more guards poured in, their hands roughly grabbing Shiel, Zev, and Finch at my side. Silver flashed as their hands were put in cuffs, and before I could summon my next breath, and with it my own glamour to protect us, silver flashed before my eyes too.

I was not cuffed however. No, the queen made sure I wasn't treated with any such dignity. The hands that reached for me didn't take my hands, they instead grabbed me by my shoulders, metal snaking around my throat as I was collared instead, the metal tightening around my skin until it made me choke.

Still, I managed to draw the smallest of breaths, a half breath really, and reached for my glamour before they could make their next move.

Only, when I reached for it this time, I couldn't find it.

I couldn't find … anything.

The hands that had collared me grabbed me and held be firm as I choked at more breath, reaching and reaching only to repeatedly find only emptiness.

It wasn't that the well within me had been run dry, it

wasn't there at all. Panic flooded through me. I had never felt so powerless before. It was as if I was stripped of everything that made me fae.

I didn't understand what was happening to me, but as my head lifted to look at the queen and the smug princess at her side, again, I knew one thing, at least.

I'd been right.

I'd guessed this might be part of the queen's plan.

But why act now? Why such urgency? The council was set to meet in a week, already. Why call them early? Was it really the riots? The talk of rebellion?

*No.*

Deep down, I knew why.

Those riots were not the first ones in this city. I'd known that the minute I first laid eyes on Rayner. What we'd witnessed was not what had sent the city into lockdown and called his emergency council.

I froze, knowing who was about the enter the council chamber the moment before he did.

Icarus.

It still wasn't until the dark fae Lord of the Wildness swept in and took the last remaining empty seat at the table that I understood.

Icarus was no longer just the Lord of the Wildness.

Icarus was now the Lord of the Northern Court, too—and there was only one way he could have convinced the queen, or any of these other new treacherous lords, to allow that.

He'd bargained for it, and I had an idea what he'd used to win his seat by their side.

"What is the meaning of this?" Shiel demanded, next. He'd fixed his advisor with a mutinous glare, but the advisor only looked to the queen. Every other eye followed, except for me.

I couldn't bring myself to look away from Icarus.

He, in turn—and for perhaps the first time—refused to look back at me. A cold shiver ran through me. Was this what Ada meant when she said I owed her nothing? Had she been trying to warn me?

Surely not.

It didn't matter though, not now. Not with the cold silver of the collar around my throat, my power somehow stripped from me just as it had now been stripped from every rightful ruler of this kingdom.

The queen straightened herself up, her shoulders pulled back as she surveyed her new council.

"This is a terrible mistake," I said, taking a step towards the queen. As soon as I did, the arms holding me tightened, restraining me in place. As if in a final act of treachery, I recognized the tumble of red hair falling over my captor's shoulders. I swiveled slightly, twisted between the hands that held me until my uncle was forced to meet my eye. "Now is not the time for a coup. Our kingdom is in danger."

All I earned in response was a dismissive hiss from the queen.

"Did you not see the riots last night? I did," I gasped, turning back to her. "I was there."

"They're humans, we're fae, they'll fall in line," the queen said. "They're always upset about something or other. This too will pass."

"Not from the humans," I said, despite my uncle's tightening grip. "From fae."

"Fae?"

The queen's eyebrow rose.

"From Avarath."

She let out a laugh that was soon mirrored by the other lords seated before her. When she sobered up enough to speak, the pity in her voice was enough to make a new layer of rage awaken in me.

"The veil between our realms hasn't been crossed in centuries, silly girl. If you were truly fae, you'd know that. But just as I told you …" she said, gesturing to all gathered before us. "She's nothing but an imposter. She might have the king's blood running through her veins, but she's not one of us."

Shiel's advisor nodded, one hand slamming down on the table in agreement. "It's about time we were finished with that old king's line, anyway. No one fae should have that much power."

"And now that my daughter has mastered the new glamour enough to create her own version on Tongues, then that will be enough to keep the people happy," the queen agreed.

I swallowed, hard, as I watched my world crumble before me. I'd known the queen planned something, some kind of treachery, but never this. It was one thing to depose me, to join the scrabble for power in the old king's absence, but to ignore the true danger staring us in the face?

That was madness. That was the surest way to make sure that terrible vision of bodies I couldn't banish came to pass.

"But the prophecy …" I started again.

"The prophecy has been in place through more storms than this," Icarus said, cutting me off. Only then did his gaze finally turn to fix on me. "Whatever comes our way, we will weather it. But war?"

His use of the word *storm* wasn't lost on me. But this time, it was a slap in the face. "Now that you're in chains, there'll be no war."

And that was the second.

The other heads around the table nodded in agreement.

How was this happening? How were they all so stupid?

I wanted to argue, to tell them what Icarus had confided in me. This was his plan, this was what he wanted. He'd told me.

*I'm here to start a war, My Storm.*

Icarus' words echoed in my ears once more as the queen ordered me dragged out alongside Shiel and his men. As I looked at the dark fae once more, betrayal wrapping its fingers around my tender heart, I knew I had no right to feel the way I did. I'd ignored his words because of what came after. But I should have been listening.

He'd warned me.

He'd told me what he was about to do.

Knowing that still did nothing to soften the blow. His plan was falling into place, one court at a time.

And now I was helpless to stop it.

# A NOTE FROM THE AUTHOR

Welcome back to A Court of Thieves and Traitors. One last part to go.

We hope you've loved the first few parts of Aurra's story. The next part of Aurra's story will be available for preorder soon on Amazon.

For more books set in the same world as A Court of Thieves and Traitors, check out A Veil of Truth and Trickery, Book One of Analeigh's bestselling series, The Veiled Realm, also available on Amazon!

If you enjoyed The Queen The Fae Forgot please consider leaving a review!

With Love,

Analeigh (Eden) & Sabrina

*Abandon*

ALSO BY SABRINA THATCHER

**A Coven of Fangs**

*Vampire Captivated*

*Vampire Compelled*

*Vampire Coveted*

**Feral Mates**

*Alpha Rejected*

*Alpha Rising*

*Alpha Returned*

Printed in Great Britain
by Amazon